THE HEIRESS OF ROTHMORE HALL

By

Micah Cozzens

THE HEIRESS OF ROTHMORE HALL

by Micah Cozzens

Table of Contents

Artwork

The cover art was created by Paul Garcia, whose other work can be found at   https://paul_design.artstation.com/. Many thanks for his excellent work.

Acknowledgements

This book would not exist without the support and excellent advice given by my writing group, including Taisha, Michael, Lindsey, Ranae, and Rebecca. Many thanks for your guidance and reading.

Chapter One: The News

The news that Marianne Keyes had been left ten thousand pounds by her late great-uncle swept the village of Dair so quickly, she was the last to hear about it. The letter announcing this strange twist of fortune—authored by one Blandish E. Poole, solicitor—had arrived a week prior. But, like many letters delivered to busy families, it went unopened until breakfast on an obscure Tuesday, when Mrs. Keyes, wife of a rector and therefore always busy with something, only sat down to read it when the eggs were safely plattered.

"Mr. Keyes," Mrs. Keyes said.

Mr. Keyes, absorbed in his eggs, didn't answer.

"Mr. Keyes!" Mrs. Keyes said.

"Yes, dear?" he said, emerging from his breakfast.

She handed him the letter with hands that were not entirely steady.

He read it and his eyes followed hers to Marianne, who was absorbed in her toast.

Marianne Keyes was the third of seven daughters. Twenty-four years old, a voracious reader of novels, a moderately good cook, and a decent seamstress—she had no other defining virtues. At least, none that could explain why, when her parents told her that she was now the inheritor of ten thousand pounds, her great-uncle would have chosen her.

Her father said, "Marianne, read this letter. It's about you."

Marianne read it and, speechless, set it against a platter of boiled eggs. "Great Uncle Babbage left me ten thousand pounds?"

Her younger sister Sophie, always eager to puncture an older sister's ego, piped up: "But Mama, Great Uncle didn't even know Marianne."

"Hush, Soph," Mrs. Keyes said. "He must have. He's left her his fortune." She turned to her third daughter, as if hoping her guess would be verified.

But Marianne too was baffled. "I only spoke to him once," she said. "And only then to say I admired his collection from the East."

"In Hampstead?" Mrs. Keyes said.

Marianne nodded. Her youngest sister, Penelope, was happily ignorant of the conversation and had reached over to eat her older sister's unattended toast. Marianne watched the theft with uncharacteristic passivity. Her other younger sisters, Evie and Anne, had stopped eating and were staring, open-mouthed. Marianne could clearly see Anne's half-masticated eggs.

"What else did he say to you, then?" Mrs. Keyes asked.

"Nothing," Marianne said, wracking her brains. "He said the weather was hot and that he hoped I wasn't a fool, and I said I wasn't, and he asked me 'Did I like to read' and I said yes and when he asked me what I was reading, I said 'The Monk' and he started roaring with laughter and then he asked what a girl like me was doing, reading such a book, and I said I liked it and—" Marianne felt herself rambling and stopped short.

Mrs. Keyes tsked. "I always felt that book was too much for such a young girl. Ghosts and carryings-on and such."

"Carryings-on and such" was Mrs. Keyes' way of referring to sex.

"You never even read it, Mama," Marianne said.

"I've heard about it," Mrs. Keyes said. Then she remembered the letter and her daughter's ten thousand pounds. "I'll wager that's why he did it," she said with a sigh. "You made the old man laugh. No one else ever could."

"But I didn't do it intentionally," Marianne said. "It was an accident."

"Marianne's got ten thousand pounds by accident?" Soph said.

"She has," Mrs. Keyes said.

"Can I get ten thousand pounds by accident?" Soph said.

Mrs. Keyes paused, about to deliver a sharp "No," but she couldn't quite do it. Because after the events of the last twenty-four hours, who was she to say what was and wasn't possible?

When Marianne left with her sisters later to go about the usual chores of the parish, Mrs. Keyes and Mr. Keyes remained at the table.

Mrs. Keyes asked her husband, "Do you think it was some sort of trick? Uncle always did have a wicked sense of humor."

"If it is, then the joke has cost him ten thousand pounds," Mr. Keyes said.

"John?" Mrs. Keyes said.

"Yes?"

"That's a lot of money, isn't it?" Mrs. Keyes knew that it was. Why did she ask? Because she needed to hear aloud what her husband then said, to confirm what she already felt to be true—

"It's a life-changing amount of money," Mr. Keyes said. "Marianne will be rich beyond belief."

"And us?" Mrs. Keyes said.

"We will remain as we always have," Mr. Keyes said.

"Oh, I hope this doesn't change her too much," Mrs. Keyes said.

Mr. Keyes didn't say what he was thinking: How could that amount of money not change someone?

By the time Marianne was loaded into a carriage with her father, bound for London and the offices of Blandish E. Poole, solicitor, she had begun to think about what a sum of this amount meant. She could have done more thinking, of course, had her mother not turned the house upside down with frantic preparations, which required, as Mrs. Keyes put it, "all hands either scrubbing, stitching, or stirring."

Mrs. Keyes, who herself had known the sting of being underdressed in London society, determined that "no one was going to call her Marianne a poor country girl" and set about sewing a new set of clothes in record time. Mr. Keyes, seeing the bill for the fabric, grumbled—

"My dear, you know we haven't gotten the money yet. Are you determined to bankrupt us?"

But Mrs. Keyes couldn't hear him or, indeed, anyone. She was driven on by the relentless work ethic of a woman trying to outrun her anxieties. She constructed not only a new wardrobe, but also set about making Marianne presentable in other ways, some of which worked. She sent Marianne up the hill to stay an afternoon with her older sister Ruth who had been to London most recently of all of them. Ruth had been apprised of her younger sister's strange fortune and was left to try to convey to Marianne, in one afternoon, all of what might be expected of her in London. Ruth had married early and well and spent her days managing her children and perusing the garden. Over the course of a few hours, while tending to a sick son and daughter, as well as two other children, she tried to explain to Marianne what a ball was, how to act at the theater, and how London differed from Dair. The result was such chaos that Marianne was left to return to her parents' house more confused than before.

Mrs. Keyes took no notice. She was in a race against time. She enlisted the help of her other daughter, Judith, who had moved too far away for visiting, but who could correspond. Judith, perhaps stunned by the news and herself the wife of a busy clergyman, managed only to write that Marianne had better "mind her manners" among the "London set."

Armed with such vague advice, what was Marianne to do? She would have preferred to sit and read and daydream of her new life, but her mother was having none of that. In every moment Marianne was not sleeping or eating, Mrs. Keyes had her stitching. The dress patterns, taken from a book borrowed from the richest family in the parish, were more complex than any Mrs. Keyes had attempted before, but she was a determined woman. She tasked Soph with minding Penelope, and had her other daughters, Evelyn and Rachel, pack Marianne's trunk. But never satisfied with the results, Mrs. Keyes eventually sent them out to play and did it herself.

Finally, on the eve of their departure, when even Mrs. Keyes had to admit there was nothing more she could do, she pronounced Marianne "ready."

Marianne did not feel ready. Unbending from her stoop, in which she had sat, furiously sewing for the last week, Marianne had collapsed into the bed she shared with Evelyn and fallen promptly asleep, only to wake with her mother shaking her, saying that the carriage had arrived. It was time to go.

Marianne washed, dressed quickly, kissed a sleepy Evie goodbye, and was made by her mother to eat something. Her mother fussed over her hair so long that Mr. Keyes was forced to tell her, gently, "My dear, the coachman won't wait forever."

They were then settled into a coach, which smelled too much like the horses pulling it, and Mrs. Keyes' last words to her daughter were: "Eat these pears before they get overripe." And she pushed a basket of pears into her daughter's lap.

They were halfway down the road when, with a sigh, Mr. Keyes said, "Your mother's only flaw, Marianne, is that she never was very good at farewells."

Was that what this was? Marianne thought. A farewell? That word sounded so hideous and dramatic.

"But I'll be coming back," she said.

Her father didn't respond directly, and only said, "This money will change everything for us, Marianne."

When he said "us," Mr. Keyes didn't mean that he himself would benefit from the inheritance. Rather, he was a father who saw his daughter as largely an extension of himself—not in the way of a tyrant, but in the way that love always insists on connecting people, even when age or distance threatens the connection. Truth be told, Marianne was, if not Mr. Keyes' favorite daughter, certainly the daughter he most depended on. She was a good reader and he liked talking with her about books. While it had always been expected that Rebecca and Ruth would marry young, the same could not have been said for Marianne. Mr. Keyes had always had an unspoken expectation that Marianne would not marry and would remain at home for the rest of his life. He had, in his secret heart of hearts, derived some comfort from this vision of stability. He would never, of course, have prevented her from marrying had she chosen. But his third daughter had never expressed interest in any man and no man had ever expressed interest in her. He had perhaps had visions of Marianne feeding him and Mrs. Keyes tea in their old age, tending to them as their life neared its close.

But now—he couldn't reasonably expect that, could he?

And then, with the abruptness of lightning, a rather disturbing thought came to him—As an heiress, Marianne would perhaps be a desirable conquest.

Mr. Keyes, over the noise of the carriage, attempted something like a fatherly warning: "You'll have to mind the men of London, Marianne."

"What?" Marianne said. She was regretting not eating all the food her mother had put on her plate and was suddenly hungry.

"The men of London can smell an heiress a mile away," her father said.

Marianne, not grasping that she was the heiress in this situation, had only said, "Oh."

And Mr. Keyes, unable to talk to any of his daughters about anything even verging on romance, left it at that.

The journey to London took several days, which necessitated staying at several undesirable lodging houses, and it left Marianne with a bad impression of her new life. If having ten thousand pounds meant breakfasting with strangers, sleeping in a strange bed, and being in a carriage all day, then she wasn't sure it was for her.

But Marianne was twenty-four years old and had some latent spirit of adventure. She liked seeing the countryside roll away as they progressed nearer and nearer to London—to think that she, Marianne Keyes, who has never been anywhere or done anything, was going to London to meet with a solicitor! It was very exciting.

She asked, in a flare of spirit, for some paper at a lodging house, which was reluctantly given to her by a sour-faced woman. Marianne had one friend in the whole world, besides her sisters: Madelyn Tolbert, whose father, a missionary, had been briefly in Dair some five years ago. Madelyn and Marianne had corresponded ever since, although less often lately. The Tolberts' frequent travels meant that they were rarely at one address for long.

Marianne wrote to her friend with a sort of girlish buoyancy she would have been embarrassed for her father to see—

Madelyn, she wrote, in a rather fine, though unsteady hand, it seems I have come into a sudden wealth. My great-uncle, the war hero and recluse, died and we've learned he left his money to me. No one knows why. Unless it was because I once made him laugh so hard his wig fell off. Do you remember me talking about my great-uncle? I think I will buy a lot of oranges and paper and chocolates—and I will be a fine lady and go to the theater.

Marianne wrote then about her poor, needle-pricked hands and other details of the preparations for London before finding herself saying, at the end of the letter, I worry I won't be very good at being rich. Then before she could cross it out, she had the letter addressed and sent.

Their arrival in London was heralded by the worst weather the city had seen in a year, with torrential rains. Mr. Keyes had to shield Marianne with his overcoat as they dashed into the office that they were told, by their impatient coachman, belonged very definitely to Mr. Blandish E. Poole. Marianne, aside from being drenched, was tired, hungry, and hot. Having never previously traveled, the experience had left her excited and frightened in equal measures.

Mr. Keyes, however, was a self-possessed man and calmly asked to be seen by Mr. Poole. Marianne was tempted to wring out her bonnet but before she could, a short little man with beautiful blue eyes rounded the corner and identified them.

"So you must be Mr. Keyes!" he said and ushered them into his office, a warm and well-appointed room with furniture that Marianne intuitively knew was expensive.

Mr. Poole talked to Mr. Keyes very amiably about their travels, the coachman, the weather they had seen, the English countryside. When these niceties were completed, a silence pervaded the room. Marianne was somehow both sweating and cold, although she wasn't sure how that was possible.

"We should address, then, the business that has brought you from your hamlet to London," Mr. Poole said.

"Yes," Mr. Keyes said.

Mr. Poole has documents spread before him on his large desk. "It must have been a shock to you when you learned that your daughter was named sole heiress to Gerald Babbage's estate."

"He had no children?" Mr. Keyes said. Why he asked, Marianne didn't know. Her father knew Great Uncle Babbage had no children.

"No," Mr. Poole said. "At least, none in this country." They exchanged a significant glance that confused Marianne.

"I was a bit surprised, yes," Mr. Keyes said. "My daughter claims to have had no correspondence with or, indeed, significant connection to the man."

"The will of Mr. Baggage," Mr. Poole said, "was highly unusual. But it is all legal and above board. I made sure of that myself. Would you like to hear it?"

"Yes," Mr. Keyes said. He glanced at Marianne, who nodded.

Mr. Poole put on his glasses and began:

"The will of Mr. Gerald Baggage names as sole heiress a Miss Marianne Keyes, daughter of niece Mary Keyes. It may perhaps confuse my good family as to why I have chosen this girl to inherit my considerable assets. Let it be no mystery: I chose her because she made me laugh, once, harder than I had laughed in many years, and that is no small thing for a man of my years."

"So it was because of that!" Marianne said.

Mr. Poole fixed her with a look and Marianne fell silent immediately.

"May I continue?" Mr. Poole said.

"Yes," Marianne said, duly chastened.

"The will goes on to state," Mr. Poole said, "the conditions of the inheritance."

Marianne and her father leaned forward in their seats. Marianne had not even considered that there might be conditions!

"I wish," Mr. Poole read aloud, "for my heiress to reside in my family estate, Rothmore. She will find the castle old but serviceable. It was a good home to me in my later years and also serves as the burial place of my late wife, may she rest in peace. I wish for a young woman to live there, to brighten it with her presence, and to restore it to its former glory."

Brighten it with her presence? Marianne wasn't sure what that meant. Was she supposed to plant flowers or something? She wished now that she had paid more attention to her mother's work in the garden.

Mr. Poole continued reading. "Furthermore, the inheritance is to be apportioned out annually, over a period of ten years, in the sum of five hundred pounds a year, with the remaining sum being delivered in the tenth year." He shot Marianne a sharp, blue-eyed glance.

Marianne, to whom the sum of five hundred sounded as great as ten thousand, only nodded. Maybe her great-uncle had intended to prevent her from spending all the money at once.

"He also says," Mr. Poole noted, "that he wishes you to take especial care of his private collection, which you will find in the library."

"Collection of what?" Marianne asked.

"He doesn't specify," Mr Poole said.

Collection of coins? Sabers? War memorabilia? Marianne envisioned shelves of dusty artifacts.

"Where is Rothmore?" Mr. Keyes asked.

"West of London," Mr. Poole said. "No great distance."

That did not assure Mr. Keyes, who was certain that Rothmore was, at the very least, a great distance from his parish.

"He has included," Poole said, "letters that will prove the validity of the inheritance and a key to the room containing the aforementioned collection." He slid these items across his large desk. Marianne held the key and noted its heft.

"The head housekeeper, a Mrs. Grubert, will be there to welcome you upon your arrival," Mr. Poole said. "It's all been arranged."

"But surely, for a girl of her age to live alone in that setting," Mr. Keyes ventured, "is highly unusual."

"The house is hers to do with as she wishes," Mr. Poole said. "But a condition of the inheritance is that Marianne resides in the house. Unusual or no, it was my client's wish."

Mr. Keyes was conflicted. To send his daughter off to an unknown house, far from the only home she had ever known, was fraught with uncertainty. What would Mrs. Keyes say, when she heard that her third daughter was now sole resident of Rothmore, a lone woman in an isolated estate? What if something happened?

But what would happen to her? Mr. Keyes didn't know. He envisioned a gothic manor falling apart at the seams, taking Marianne with it, but even he had to admit that such a threat was rather vague and insubstantial.

"She will have servants?" Mr. Keyes said.

"Loyal servants," Mr. Poole said. "And I can vouch myself for the groundskeeper, Hamish. He's helped me on many a pheasant hunting venture. He's a good sort, very reliable. And devoted, you know, to the family name. Marianne will come to no harm while Hamish is there."

"I can do it, Papa," Marianne said, with more confidence than she really felt. "I'm not about to give up ten thousand pounds just because I won't live in an older house." She tried to make the whole situation sound sweet and domestic, not strange and unusual. But of course it was just that—strange and unusual. Perhaps that had been part of Great Uncle Babbage's plan—a final laugh, to puzzle them all with strange requests.

Mr. Keyes nodded, which Mr. Poole took as consent. "Very good," Poole said. "I'll have you sign—" He produced a series of truly massive documents which he had Mr. Keyes and Marianne sign. When this was finally done, Marianne's hand was aching and her mind was on her stomach. She was hungry.

Her father said goodbye to Mr. Poole, who took the chance to inform them of other particulars—how Marianne would receive the annual allowance, what further documentation would need to be completed, and when Marianne was expected at Rothmore. The date was sooner than she had expected: within the week. She felt her nerves increase. So she wouldn't have time to return home from London before going to Rothmore. She had hoped, briefly, that she might. But mostly Marianne was hungry and her father, no doubt also feeling his stomach, had them conveyed to the house of an Oxford friend, a Mr. Bell, someone he had known thirty years before. When they arrived, her father greeted his old friend and they fell into old conversations about parish life and politics, so completely that Mr. Keyes rather forgot about Marianne.

Marianne, meanwhile, was left to Mrs. Bell, who eyes her shrewdly and said, "So you're the girl who's got all the town talking, with your ten thousand pounds."

"Talking?" Marianne said. "Who's talking?"

Mrs. Bell put some bread and a savory stew on the table, which Marianne ate eagerly.

"It's well known," Mrs. Bell said. "Mr. Babbage's affairs were a source of curiosity to many people. Why people care about other people's business is, of course, beyond me," she sniffed derisively to show that she was not one to succumb to such temptation, "but care, they do." She wagged a finger at Marianne and said, "If I were you, I'd be careful. There's many people who'd like to get their hands on ten thousand pounds."

"How?" Marianne said. "I don't have it now. They couldn't steal it from me."

"There are some who would trick you out of it or," Mrs. Bell said slyly, "Or marry you for it."

"Oh no," Marianne said through a mouthful of bread. "I won't marry."

"If you keep eating like that, you won't," Mrs. Bell said.

Marianne felt the urge to hiss, like a feral cat. Her poor eating etiquette was a source of tension between her and her mother. Mrs. Keyes always despaired of her failure to teach Marianne how to wield a spoon like a lady.

Marianne wished now that she had taken her mother's lessons more to heart. Now she was supposed to be a lady and mistress of an estate, but she didn't even know how to hold her spoon.

"Am I a grand lady now?" Marianne asked.

"Money doesn't make you a lady," Mrs. Bell said. "Only poise and good breeding can do that." Marianne nodded. "But," Mrs. Bell said, "money helps. It helps a lot."

Mr. and Mrs. Bell insisted for Mr. Keyes and Marianne to accompany them to the theater that evening. Though Marianne suspected her father would much rather have gone to bed early, he gamely agreed and Marianne, eager to see something of London society, which she could report to her sisters, began to prepare.

Her mother's dressmaking efforts hadn't been wasted and Marianne had to admit that she looked much better in her new pelisse. Almost—almost pretty. But not quite. Marianne had never been bothered that she was plain, unhandsome. She thought she looked okay and living with a rector had instilled in her a sort of culture of acceptance. If God wanted her homely, then homely she would be. There must be some purpose in it. And it had never really been a problem.

Except . . .once, when the blacksmith's boy called her ugly, and threw a rotten plum at her and it left a streak across her cheek. She had been so angry at him that when she had scrubbed the juice stains off her pinafore, she had imagined, while kneading the fabric clean, that she was strangling him. It hadn't been a very Christian thought, but she hadn't felt Christian that day. She had felt furious.

And yes, once she had been ignored during every dance at the parish hall. It had been her first dance. She had asked and asked her mother to be allowed to go. And then, she hadn't been asked to dance even once. She had tried not to let it bother her. No one else had even noticed, which soothed her (thank God no one else had noticed!) and also angered her (how could no one not notice her embarrassment? Her shame? Did no one care?) After that, she simply hadn't gone to dances. Her mother and father had commented on it once, that Marianne must have preferred the company of her books. And Marianne never corrected them. She did like books. But mostly she just didn't want to be embarrassed again.

Now, staring at herself in a new dress—blue, with embroidered flowers—she felt almost, almost pretty, and Marianne smiled at herself in the glass and imagined herself as a grand lady in a grand manor. She was going to have fun tonight. She swore she was going to have fun tonight.

They left for the theater around eight, in a carriage that Mr. and Mrs. Bell had hired. Marianne saw in her father a tiredness but also a sort of youthful enthusiasm that always came out when he was around old Oxford friends. She herself was a mix of nerves and anticipation. It was all she could do to keep her foot from tapping the carriage floor in an annoying rhythm.

When they arrived at Drury Lane, the bustle and commotion of carriages was so overwhelming, Marianne almost thought they had come upon docks or some bustling shipyard. (Not that she had ever seen a bustling shipyard—but she'd read books, and in books, there were bustling shipyards.)

Mrs. Bell must have seen Marianne's shock at the commotion, because she laughed. "My, what an adorable country bumpkin you are!" she said. "Mr. Keyes, you should have introduced your daughter to society a little earlier! She's a scared rabbit."

Mr. Keyes, who had been engaged in a theological debate with Mr. Bell, looked over briefly, nodded politely, then returned to the discussion.

Mrs. Bell rolled her eyes and said to Marianne, "Come on, dear. We'll have to get out of here. We won't be able to get any closer to the door. Not with these crowds."

Marianne was handed down to Mr. Bell, who had clambered out of the carriage first.

"Mind your feet," Mrs. Bell said. "The horses have been here."

The street did indeed present evidence of horses—big, steaming, stinking piles of evidence. But Marianne wasn't going to let that tarnish her theater experience. Sure, the theater wasn't all glamour. The stench made that apparent. But she hadn't even been inside yet. Pushed between elbows and women's skirts, Marianne got only a glimpse of a stucco facade, illuminated unevenly in torchlight.

But the inside of the theater did not disappoint.

Inside the lobby were more people, a cacophony of smells, but also large mirrors in the walls that reflected the opulent bustling of people determined to look their best. Marianne fought the urge to panic and, though twenty-four and definitely an adult woman, felt tempted to seize her father's hand for comfort. She resisted. She was a great lady now and great ladies didn't need to hold hands.

She tried to hold her head up and look posh, but all artifice was driven from her when they passed through the entrance to the interior of the theater. And Marianne audibly gasped.

The theater was massive, with stacked boxes in which people were crammed. The floor was just as crowded, full of jostling people in varying degrees of finery. The ceiling was gleaming, an ornate pattern meant, she suspected, to dazzle and confuse in equal measures.

Mr. Bell guided them to seats on the floor. "Maria will be singing tonight," he said.

Ashamed to own her ignorance in front of Mr. Bell, Marianne whispered to Mrs. Bell, "Who?"

"Maria Raliban," Mrs. Bell said. "Only the most famous opera singer in London. You'll see, she has a voice to shatter heaven's gates."

Marianne nodded, unsure if that was a good or a bad thing.

After an interminable wait, the opera finally started and Marianne learned that Maria Raliban did indeed have a voice to shatter heaven's gates. Marianne was made impatient by the heat of the room and the lack of shifting space, but she survived by clinging to Maria Raliban's voice, a life raft in a strange and foreign place.

At intermission, Mrs. Bell turned to Marianne, who had begun sweating, and said, "Well?"

Marianne could only say, "She has a rare talent." She had no idea if it really was a rare talent, but Mrs. Bell seemed to take her seriously and nodded approvingly.

Overcome by an urge both to hug Ms. Raliban and also to towel off the sweat now pouring down her back and arms, Marianne asked, "Where do I—" She wasn't sure the right way to say it.

Mrs. Bell, sensing what Marianne wanted, took her by the hand. "Follow me. Of course, the line will be long at intermission, but that's to be expected. We'll be back," she said to Mr. Bell and Mr. Keyes, both of whom nodded in their general direction. (They had been distracted for several minutes because they were trying to determine if a bald gentleman was someone they'd known in their school days. It was difficult to know because, of course, back then he'd had hair.)

Marianne was guided by Mrs. Bell into the bowels of the theater, past women congregating in little groups, some of whom looked at her, most of whom didn't. But those who did look at her seemed to do so knowingly, as if she had something on her dress. A stain, maybe. Was something wrong with her?

After getting precious moments in front of a glass, which she used to surreptitiously wipe her forehead, Marianne went into the foyer to await Mrs. Bell, or rather, a room that served as an in-between to the foyer, a room in which women had draped hats and coats and coverings. It was there, as Marianne was just claiming a bare spot on a red couch, that she heard it.

Male voices, approaching, presumably heading outside. "My God," one voice said. "There's not a single pretty woman here tonight."

"Some weren't bad looking," another said.

"That's because you're nearly blind, George," another said.

"Did you see that creature in the row behind us?" a third voice said.

"What, the one in the blue?"

"That's the one."

"What a sight she was," the third said.

"Beside that old clergyman, too," the first said. "God, George, sometimes I envy your blindness. You're spared sight at the most convenient times."

The voices faded down the hallway, leaving Marianne in a state of emotional freefall.

Marianne did not possess a feeble mind or even a particularly vain personality. She had no great ambition to be beautiful or to attract anyone. But after such a strange week, and while wearing her new dress which she and her mother had labored so long on, she had wanted to be thought decent. If not beautiful, then at least decent.

But she had been called a creature, a sight, and a motivation for blindness.

And yes, Marianne was certain those voices had been discussing her. What other clergyman had been present? What other woman in a blue dress had been seated beside such a clergyman? No, it was her they meant. There was no escaping the insult through self-deception or telling herself they had been discussing some other, unfortunate woman.

She was the object of scorn. She, and her stupid blue dress.

She found that she was tearing up and she wiped her eyes on the back of her hand. The tears seemed unusually warm, unusually fat, and they fell eagerly.

It wouldn't have stung so much had they not sounded so refined. Because they did sound refined—cruel and young, but also refined. They spoke in the tidy, neat accents of—she hated to think it, but it was true—of her father. And she knew her father was an educated man.

To be called ugly by uneducated men was one thing. To be deemed "a creature" by educated men was somehow worse. But, as Marianne was learning, cruelty didn't abide by class divisions.

She struggled to steady her hands, clenching in them fistfuls of the blue dress. Her mother had worked hard on this dress. And with thirty seconds of conversation, its beauty had evaporated for Marianne. She was tempted strongly to tear it off and walk into the street naked. But better sense prevailed and she managed to rein in herself with deep breaths and the knowledge that she had to get through the next two hours without showing any signs of emotional distress. Otherwise, her father or Mrs. Bell would ask if she was all right, and she would have to lie, and Marianne didn't want to lie, because she knew that if she did, she would inevitably begin to cry. And Marianne couldn't cry.

With prayers and implications to God that she be allowed to keep herself together, Marianne managed to squash her embarrassment and wounded pride into a ball at the back of her throat. When Mrs. Bell returned, asking if Marianne was ready to return to their seats, Marianne was able to reply, with a perfectly even tone, that "Yes, she was."

She kept an expression of mild, if distant, interest through the rest of the performance, through the jostling back outside, through the carriage ride back to the Bells' home, until the moment the door shut and she was alone in the room allocated for her use. Only then did Marianne cry. Afterward, Marianne splashed her eyes with cold water, in a gesture at self control, and she lay down to sleep. She imagined that the people to whom those three voices belonged, the voices who had insulted her, were phantoms, maybe ghosts of the theater who existed to torment its patrons. Maybe they were poltergeists of some sort. Maybe her father could have exorcised the cruelty from them, had he come in a clerical capacity. The thought of her father reading a bible at the walls of the theater made Marianne smile, and when she dreamed, the dreams were pleasant, if jumbled.

Marianne's stay in London recovered from her disappointment at the theater, and she enjoyed the next days. Mrs. Bell took her to London bookshops, where Marianne was able to purchase books she knew wouldn't make their way to sleepy little Dair for a year. She purchased so many, in fact, that her father grumbled, "Marianne, you don't have the inheritance yet." But Marianne was, as Mrs. Bell assured her, a lady now, and ladies bought books. Ladies also bought hats and shoes and ribbons and lace. (The lace was, Marianne had to admit, a very costly purchase.)

At the end of the week, Marianne did get a portion of her inheritance. She was taken to a very large and imposing bank, where her father and Mr. Poole and she were made to sign yet more documents, and she was given an allowance and instructed that, if she wished to send for more money before the end of the year, she had only to write to Mr. Poole, who would supply it for her. But her spending would not, according to the contract she had signed, exceed five hundred pounds per annum. Marianne left the bank with money in a bag, tucked inside a pocket, which felt heavier than it should have. She had never had any money of her own.

Marianne could not imagine needing such a sum, but Mrs. Bell, who liked to give off a sense of worldly wisdom that was mostly justified, said, "You'd be surprised at how fast such a sum disappears when you're trying to maintain a household. How your poor mother has managed to raise seven girls on your father's income is a question of modern-day miracles."

"My father does well enough," Marianne said.

"But you'll do better," Mrs. Bell said, and while Marianne knew it was true, the statement scared her. She had never imagined having more money than her father.

But Marianne couldn't be too angry at Mrs. Bell. Without her, Marianne would have been lost in London. Her father remembered the city from two decades previous and knew then only the destinations a clergyman cared for. But Mrs. Bell knew the tea rooms, the haberdasheries, and where to buy enough parchment and ink to keep Marianne in good letter-writing supply for a year. But Marianne's favorite trip was to a small shop to purchase cocoa—something Marianne had never had, and the aroma of which pleased her so much, it was all she could do to keep from spending all her money on it right then and there. But Mrs. Bell talked her into getting a small, sensible sample, and Marianne was left longing for more.

Finally, the day arrived. Marianne and her father had to leave.

Hugging Mrs. Bell goodbye was harder than Marianne had anticipated. It was like saying goodbye to her mother for a second time and Marianne was surprised to feel herself blinking away yet more tears when they parted.

But the true tears didn't come until she and her father had ridden the ten miles from London, where the road to Dair and Rothmore forked.

Mr. Keyes helped the coachman arrange Marianne's things in a different coach, bound north, and they sat, saying nothing, until it became clear that they had to go or risk missing their journey altogether.

Mr. Keyes was silent, torn between two duties. He needed to return to his parish. He had been away for too long already. But to send Marianne to an unknown estate, in who knows what state of repair, and for potentially years, was beyond him.

But he looked at her and saw some solid understanding, some good sense, and, most of all, the same daughter he had raised. He could not deny that he had done well in raising her.

"Goodbye, Marianne," he said, and his voice sounded feeble, even to him.

He hugged her, then, and Marianne didn't cry until she was secure in the coach. Then, hiding her eyes behind her sleeve, she cried for the next ten miles.

If inheriting ten thousand pounds was so wonderful, so miraculous, then why was it making her cry so frequently, three times in the space of a single week?

Chapter Two: Seeking an Heiress

Richard awoke on a Tuesday with no particular plans to seek an heiress. But plans change over the course of a day.

He woke to find himself still in the previous night's clothes, with a head aching and a banging on the door.

George and Arthur were also asleep, and also roused by the noise.

"Make it stop," Arthur groaned, burying his head with a mop of very curly hair beneath a pillow.

George, all but blind without his glasses, blinked confusedly around the room. "What time is it?"

"I'll get it," Richard said, bleary and sore. He'd slept on his neck all wrong. He craved water anyway, and a piss, and shuffled to the door, which he flung open to reveal a very unhappy looking Abigail Kent, daughter of the merchant from whom they were renting this room.

"Abigail," Richard said, trying his best to look charming, which was hard because he really had a headache. "You could tempt a painter to his brush today. Your eyes—"

"Hush with all that," Abigail said, blushing nonetheless. "I've come to tell you you've got to go. You've missed your two weeks' payment, and my brother and father won't let you say any longer."

"Abigail, have pity," Richard said. "We're just three young artists in need of a room. We'll have the money for you soon. Business is just a little slower than usual this time of year."

"You've been saying that for the last month," Abigail said. "It won't work this time."

"You have a hard heart," Richard said. "You must have, to speak so to someone so devoted to you."

"Stop flattering," Abigail said. "You're to be out by the end of the day. Otherwise my father will have such a fit—"

Richard could feel the situation escaping him and tried to rescue the conversation. He smiled wider, hoping last night's food was not visible in his teeth. "Sweet Abigail," he said, "I'll write a poem for your kindness if you'd only give us as much kindness as you're capable of."

Abigail sighed. "My father won't—"

Richard seized her arm. "Abigail, think of the good times we've had."

"Me harassing you for money or you vomiting in the stairs?" she said.

"I for one have enjoyed our little tete-a-tetes," Richard said.

Abigail sighed. "Be out by the end of the week. Otherwise, my father will murder you himself." And she looked at him with hesitation. "And when are you going to write that poem about me?"

"Soon, soon," Richard said.

Abigail nodded and disappeared down the stairs with a flounce.

Richard sighed and deflated against the doorway. "Well, boys," he said. "It may be time to seek another establishment."

"I heard," George said. "Even your charms expire, it seems."

"Or I'm not as charming as I think I am," Richard said.

"That seems more likely," Arthur said, voice muffled by the pillow, which was still sandwiching his head.

Richard closed the door and found himself in a too familiar situation.

"Do we have any money?" he asked.

"No," Arthur said.

"Do we have anywhere left to go?" Richard asked.

"No," Arthur said.

"Do we have any kind of a plan?" Richard asked.

"No," George and Arthur said.

Richard sat down heavily on the mattress he'd been using.

"We've been chased out of Paris," Arthur said, "before that Munich, and before that Sicily. We're running out of places to be chased out of."

"I know," Richard said. "Why do you insist on stating the obvious?"

"Because all it would take for us to get out of this mess would be for you to send one letter," Arthur said. "To your mother, if your father won't answer. Beg for money, promise them to reform, and then we can leave for the Continent."

"No," Richard said.

"But think—" Arthur said.

"No," Richard said, and he left the room, intending to swill himself in the room provided for that purpose. He also left the room, however, to avoid Arthur or George reading on his face the truth, which was this:

In London, Richard had hoped, privately, for some miraculous reconciliation with his parents. Hearing news of his mother being in town, he had sent a letter to her asking for a meeting. In return, he had gotten, not a letter from his mother, but a stern letter from his father in which he said a reconciliation was not possible, not desired, and Richard was, in other words, on his own.

Staring at the four square inches of glass in the lavatory, Richard tried to explain, to himself, how he had gotten here.

Richard Lowell was not a particularly cruel person, but he was quick to judge and always thought himself right in matters of taste. When he saw Marianne—though he did not know her to be Marianne—at the opera, he called her an unsightly creature not out of particular malice, but out of a sort of misdirected cruelty and self certainty bred of wealth, loss of wealth, and a misspent youth.

Accompanied in life and in his latest disgrace by his friends, George Gordon and Arthur Gainsborough—a distant relation of the famed painter—Richard was like many young men born to wealthy fathers: spoiled, vaguely intellectual, and full of preferences and tastes that took a significant amount of money to satisfy.

Richard differed from most men in his position, however, because of an incident that had occurred which resulted in his being cut off from his family and thus, his wealth.

As a young man at Oxford, he had experimented with everything and, in between blowing up his dormitory with a series of failed science exercises and attempting an affair with a much older, married woman, he published a series of tracts—which would have been fine, except the tracts were about the importance of atheist thought and Oxford was a religious institution. Still, all might have been fine, except Richard insisted on distributing the tracts to over a hundred of his peers, and he had listed Arthur and George as co-authors, in a rare moment of magnanimity that resulted in all three being expelled summarily.

Richard's father, who was, above all else, a businessman, could not bear the idea that his son had thrown away an expensive education to publish an ideological experiment and demanded his son change his ways or be cut off from the family and thus, his wealth. Richard was nothing if not stubborn and the conversation between father and son ended with Richard storming out of his family estate, Arthur and George in tow, Mrs. Lowell in tears, and Richard effectively impoverished.

The three young men got by at first. George's family was less willing to cut off their son than Arthur or Richard's, and so he got some money. But that money ran out quickly when Richard insisted on dragging them all to the Continent to talk philosophy in the great salons of Paris. But it became very clear very quickly that while many people sympathized with the three young men, that didn't mean anyone really wanted the expense of feeding and housing them. They bounced around from friend to friend, acquaintance to even vaguer acquaintance, wearing out their welcomes across several countries, starting and subsequently bankrupting several literary magazines, and then attempting a stint as musicians before that too ended in failure.

They had only managed the fare back to London by selling Richard's watch as a last resort and their current lodgings—a generous description of the leaking room they currently inhabited—had been secured only with charm, bribery, and a fair amount of bald-faced lying.

Richard sighed and attempted to comb his hair with his fingers. He was handsome, or he had been, but lately his peripatetic lifestyle had given a certain hardness to his features. He wasn't stupid. He knew this way of living couldn't last. They needed money, and they needed it fast.

This was when Richard, as if fated to do so, looked down at the floor. Newspapers had been spread across the site of several leaks, and Richard wasn't in the habit of reading newspapers on the floor. But today he did. What caught his eye was this:

To whom it may concern—
News has reached your esteemed authoress of a new batch of heiresses descending upon London this season who will be in want of suitable husbands.
Ms. Emilia Porchard, age sixteen, is said to like dancing and cards, to excel at the harpsichord, and to be on display for any so seeking at the coffee house on ___.
And on it went, until the final entry, which is what caught Richard Lowell's eye:
But perhaps the heiress of whom the least is known is one Ms. Marianne Keyes, heiress to the estate of her great-uncle Gerald Babbage, and who graced London with her presence last week but who has since taken up residence in her ancestral estate of Rothmore. Though appearing plain, her value to a spouse should not be underestimated, and the canny eye will see there is more here than meets the eye, approximately 10,000 more.

And with that, Richard's mind began to work.

He went back to the room and began shoving what little he had into his valise.

George said, "What's gotten into you?"

"This," Richard said, waving the sodden newspaper.

"Did you piss on that?" Arthur said.

"Disgusting," George said, with a hearty chortle.

"What? No," Richard said. "Look!"

George shoved on his glasses and Arthur raised his head. Together, they read the gossip column. "So?" George said. "It's just the usual drivel about debutantes."

"Look at that last one," Richard said.

"Marianne Keyes?" Arthur said. "Someone you know?"

"I'm about to," Richard said, knotting his cravat (which had, admittedly, seen better days) with a flourish.

"Richard," George said cautiously. "What are you up to?"

"How do I look?" Richard said.

"Like you haven't slept in twelve years," George said.

"What do you know? You're practically blind," Richard said.

Arthur ventured. "Richard, are you planning on seducing this woman for her money?"

"Obviously," Richard said.

"Do you even know this woman?" George said.

"No," Richard said. "But she also doesn't know me, which will be to our advantage. When I tell her I'm a disgraced nobleman's son looking for love, she won't know any better. I mean, read between the lines: not much is known about her, her great-uncle was a Baggage, so that means he was as daft as a doorknob. I can picture her now: some poor little dear, innocent to the ways of the world, cooped up in a grand house but longing for adventure, desperate for love but too plain to catch a husband, and then she suddenly sees me. I'm charming, humourous, regale her with tales of our adventures. She'll be eating out of the palm of my hand by Sunday. We'll be married within a month, and the money will be ours."

"This scheme of yours is riddled with flaws," George said.

"As usual," Arthur quipped.

"Suppose she has heard of you," George said. "Suppose she writes to any one of our acquaintances and learns that we have no money?"

"Or suppose you're not as charming as you think you are," Arthur said. "Or suppose she's already got someone waiting to marry her."

"All of that can be managed," Richard said. "If someone else wants her, I'll fight them. If she questions my story, I'll reassure her."

"Yes, but—" Arthur stopped.

"What?" Richard said.

"Doesn't this feel wrong?" Arthur said.

"What, morally?" Richard said.

"Yes, morally," Arthur said. "I mean, we've had some schemes before, but now we're talking about tricking a helpless young woman out of her inheritance. It seems rather unscrupulous."

"It's evil, is what it is," Richard said. "But we're desperate, aren't we? And besides, I'm an atheist, remember? I'm supposed to be unscrupulous. It goes with the title."

"Didn't you give a speech on the new morality in Vienna?" Arthur said.

"All right, all right," Richard said. "So I'm displaying a little hypocrisy—"

"A little?" Arthur said. "And why do you get to be the charming, roguish rake? I can be charming. Why not let me have a crack at the old dear?"

Richard considered. "But do you have what it takes? Do you have the utter lack of scruples and relentless perseverance necessary to make love to a woman in the interest of money?"

Arthur sighed. "I suppose not."

"Exactly," Richard said. "Let me handle this."

"Like you've handled everything else?" George said.

"But this won't be like everything else," Richard said, "because there's no way we can fail. Believe me, I know this sort of woman, I've met dozens of her type—the bored, repressed aristocrat who reads too many novels and longs to escape her lot in life, provided that escape comes in the form of a handsome man and she doesn't actually have to sacrifice anything for her principles—and I know exactly what we're getting into. Come on, let's leave before old man Kent tries to come and collect his money."

"How are we getting to Rothmore?" George said.

"We'll walk," Richard said. "Believe me, I've got this all figured out."

Arthur and George exchanged a look that suggested they had more questions, but they recognized the necessity of movement and began making ready to leave.

Richard was well out of the house, and almost to the edge of London before he really allowed himself to wonder: Did he know what he was getting himself into?

Chapter Three: Arrival at Rothmore

Marianne was jostled awake in an already jostling coach when they passed a small village, and the wheels of the coach hit stone. Looking through sleep-encrusted eyes from the window, Marianne saw a rather dull but sweet looking town, not so unlike Dair.

She wished she could ask the coachman how much farther it was to Rothmore, but Marianne was shy and couldn't get up the nerve. They had traveled all of the previous day and part of the previous day, which meant she had been thirty-six hours away from her father. That was the longest she had ever been away from any member of her family. She had spent most of the day alternating between reading—which soon resulted in a headache—and staring out the window and reviewing old letters from her friend, whose travels in Africa always read better than novels. And sometimes, her thoughts lingered on the rude comment made in the theater, which she had so unfortunately overheard. But she tried to banish that from her mind.

It was midday when the coach slowed and Marianne felt, rather than knew, that they were near her destination.

When, after a few moments, the coach stopped altogether, and she was helped out, she saw what she had already sensed.

Whatever she had pictured, Rothmore was different. She had envisioned a crumbling old estate, and Rothmore was—Rothmore was—

It was like something from a painting. It reminded her most of a gothic monastery, or what she imagined a gothic monastery might resemble. It had architectural features she couldn't even name, had never even considered that she might need to know how to name.

Her shock and awe did not impress the coachman, who bustled past and began unloading Marianne's trunks—all two of them—with brusque efficiency.

It wasn't until he had unloaded them and was about to set off again that it occurred to Marianne that some payment was required. She froze, uncertain, until she was rescued by the footsteps of someone behind her.

"Miss Marianne?" a voice said.

Marianne turned to see a woman, middle-aged, perhaps a contemporary of her mother, on the steps nearby.

"I am Marianne," Marianne said.

The woman's face broke into a smile. "I thought so. You weren't expected until tomorrow," the woman saw the coachman and said. "Go through to the inside. Your fee will be paid there."

The coachman nodded and made his way across the vast lawn.

"Let me look at you," the woman said. "I hope you don't mind my familiarity, only I heard you were a little young, and I'm a Babbage myself, on my mother's side, so in a way, we are family. Although my relatives never inherited anything so grand as the Abbey."

"Abbey?" Marianne said.

"That was the old name for it," the woman said. "Rothmore Abbey. Only your great-uncle dropped the 'Abbey'. He had no love for religion, the old villain. He called it Rothmore Hall."

"Was it an Abbey?" Marianne asked. Perhaps her sense of Gothic monasterial pasts was more correct than she knew.

"Indeed, it was," the woman said. "For four hundred years. Then, of course, Henry the Eighth changed all that, and it went to our ancestors. And a good thing for you it did, too. Come inside, then. I'll show you your home."

My home, Marianne thought. How strange, to call such a place home.

The woman said, as they passed over a vast lawn, "My name is Mrs. Grubert. I'm the housekeeper."

"You knew my great-uncle?" Marianne asked.

"For many years," Mrs. Grubert said. "Although I can't say I, or anyone else, really knew him. There was too much noise in his head for that."

Marianne didn't understand what that meant, but nodded anyway. Mrs. Grubert took her inside the house, past massive doors, and into—

"The Great Hall," Mrs. Grubert said, as Marianne looked around at a room with high ceilings, green walls, and wood panelings. A stone fireplace, not lit, occupied the center of one wall, and a large table stood in the center of the room. "This was where the monks ate, back then."

Marianne had barely registered the multitude of taxidermic trophies on the walls before Mrs. Grubert was taking her through a hall—also painted a rich green—and up a stairway. The windows had stained glass in diamonds and the railing was stone. "It looks medieval," Marianne said, when she could manage to express her awe in words.

"It is medieval," Mrs. Grubert said. Marianne felt stupid and nodded along.

They went up the stairs, which Marianne couldn't bring herself to tread too heavily on, for fear—perhaps illogically—of damaging them. Everything looked old and expensive, like something she should be viewing at a distance. Not somewhere she was actually supposed to be living. But she was meant to be living here, and so she tried to pay attention.

"Mr. Poole mentioned Uncle's collection," Marianne said. "In the library."

Mrs. Grubert nodded and turned aside to a room thick with bookshelves. Marianne had always thought her father had a lot of books, but her great-uncle had him beat. There were books on every shelf and shelves on every wall. Mrs. Grubert approached a bust of a very stern looking man and, removing it from the shelf on which it sat, revealed a compartment with a lock.

She gestured toward Marianne and Marianne realized she was expected to supply the key, which she did, fishing in her pocket for it among the parcel of money.

Mrs. Grubert inserted the key into the compartment, and unlocked its top. Marianne approached and looked down into a compartment full of—old coins?

Mrs. Grubert said, "Your great-uncle was a great collector of coinage. I expect he will have wanted you to preserve the collection."

Marianne nodded, swallowing her disappointment. She had expected something a little more exciting than currency she couldn't even use. But people had warned her that Great Uncle Babbage was eccentric. She hadn't realized a person could be eccentric and also have boring hobbies.

Mrs. Grubert closed and locked the compartment, replaced the bust, and the tour continued.

Next they stopped in a private dining room. "In his younger years, your great-uncle would entertain select numbers of guests here," Mrs. Grubert said.

Marianne saw on the table a glass, as if her great-uncle had only recently been in the room, drinking. "That glass… Is it broken?" Marianne said.

"No," Mrs. Grubert said. "It's made from the lower half of a skull. Your great-uncle found it in the east and had it fashioned into a cup."

A chill fell over Marianne and she nodded. "A human skull?"

"He never specified," Mrs. Grubert said, and the tour continued.

Marianne had to resist the urge to shudder. She would not be drinking from that cup, that was for sure. The last thing she needed was to be haunted by the ghost of a person made into a wine glass.

They moved down the hallway and into a bedroom, which Mrs. Grubert said would be Marianne's. Marianne, who had always shared a room and a bed with at least one sister, stared at the room in a sort of daze.

To say it was grand was an understatement. The bed was large and had a thick canopy with tassels. The walls were very dark, a wine red, and a table with china pitchers sat in a corner. A large window, also with tasseled curtains, admitted a generous amount of light.

Marianne was just running the back of her hand along the tassels when she saw, on steps beside the bed, a pistol.

"Mrs. Grubert?" Marianne said, pointing at the weapon. "What is that?"

It took Mrs. Grubert, who had been inspecting the amount of dust on the china pitchers, a moment to notice what Marianne was pointing at. "Your great-uncle always slept with a loaded pistol beside him," Mrs. Grubert said at last.

"Why?" Marianne said. Was there some nocturnal danger she needed to know about?

Mrs. Grubert shrugged. "I never felt it was my place to ask."

Marianne nodded, not at all assured.

Mrs. Grubert must have seen Marianne's fear, because she sighed and said, "Your great-uncle life was such that . . . I mean that his experiences had rendered him . . . paranoid."

"I see," Marianne said. "I would like the pistol removed, please."

Mrs. Grubert nodded. "Hamish will come collect it. He will also build up your fire, if you wish, before you retire."

"Yes, I would like that," Marianne said.

Marianne had also taken notice of a large portrait on the wall opposite the bed, which had a stout frame. The portrait itself was of a woman. The first thing Marianne noticed about it was the dress on the woman, which was painted with such bright, glossy strokes that the blue and silver seemed alive. The dress itself was of a much older style, with a scalloped stomacher and thick, flounced sleeves, and a skirt as dramatic as any Marianne had ever seen.

"Who is that?" Marianne asked. Mrs. Grubert followed Marianne's eyes to the portrait.

"Your Great Uncle's wife," Mrs. Grubert said.

"He was married?" Marianne said. "I never knew."

"Many years ago," Mrs. Grubert said. "She died too young."

"Of sickness?" Marianne asked.

"A kind of sickness," Mrs. Grubert said. "I wasn't here then. I was just a girl. But I heard about her death. It was a great tragedy."

Marianne noted that the portrait depicted the woman bright against a background of shadows, her head turned to the side, so she appeared to be looking at something the viewer couldn't see. She had such a far away look, such a womanish stance—one arm hanging by her side, the other against her hip.

"She is very beautiful," Marianne said.

"I met her only once," Mrs. Grubert. "But I remember her beauty. The portrait doesn't do her justice. Of course, all that was a long time ago, over fifty years."

She proceeded to direct Marianne downstairs and outside, where she pointed out statues, most of which were moldering and overgrown. Then she took Marianne to the kitchen, where, while most of the rather large room had gone untouched for years, a small corner was still in use. Marianne was given a thick dinner of potatoes and sausage, which she ate eagerly.

"Who does the cooking?" Marianne asked.

"I do," Mrs. Grubert said. "Your great-uncle had a girl from the village that came sometimes, when I was otherwise occupied. She could be secured for you, if you wish."

Marianne felt the need to clarify that she wasn't completely useless. "I can cook," Marianne said. "I know how."

"That may be," Mrs. Grubert said, "but you're now the lady of the house. It wouldn't do for you to be seen cooking."

Marianne tried to think of what a great lady would say, a lady with a medieval house. She tried to force her shoulders down to improve her posture, to smooth out the pitch of her voice.

"Then you will cook," Marianne said. "And when you are busy, I will cook. Are you busy often?" The effect was middling. Marianne sounded less confident than confused.

"Not these days," Mrs. Grubert said. "My children are all grown."

Marianne had not envisioned Mrs. Grubert with children. "I am one of seven," Marianne said, because older people tended to like those sorts of details.

Mrs. Grubert nodded. "I always wanted a girl. I only managed to have boys. Five, although Alfred died young."

"I'm sorry," Marianne said.

Mrs. Grubert seemed not to want to talk about it and the conversation turned to the maintenance of the house. Marianne learned that there was a leak in the old abbot's quarters, that it was currently being managed with a bed of straw. She also learned that Mrs. Grubert would require money in advance of each week to purchase food.

After dinner, Mrs. Grubert disappeared with a chatelaine to organize . . . something, and Marianne was left with her trunks in her new bedroom, with its large canopied bed and window, to unpack and settle in.

Hamish must have come into the room while Marianne was eating dinner, because her great-uncle's pistol was now gone.

As she unpacked her wardrobe and books, Marianne's eyes were continuously drawn to the portrait of the woman on the wall. For a portrait fifty years old, it had maintained a strange vibrance. Overcome suddenly by exhaustion, both by the day's travels, and feeling full and sleepy because of her large supper, Marianne overcame her sense of strangeness by lying on the bed. It wouldn't hurt if she lay down, just for a moment, would it? She was so tired, and the bed was so—

The next thing Marianne knew, she was awaking in a room almost entirely dark.

She instinctively reached over to feel if Evie or Soph was in the bed, but then realized that she was not at home. She was at Rothmore, in a strange bedroom. What time was it?

She blinked, rubbing her eyes. The world appeared dark. Then she saw a strip of moon on the floor. Judging by its trajectory, it was late.

Marianne struggled out of the bed and stumbled toward where she remembered the table to be. She fumbled for the candle and lit it, suffusing the room in an unsteady glow. The fire had gone out long ago, but the room was still oppressively hot and Marianne opened the window, desperate for a breeze.

She sat on the floor, and felt her eyes drawn upward to the wall, where the portrait hung.

It was late. Marianne felt she needed to be in bed, though she was not tired. Not now.

She rose, placed the candle on the table, and crawled into bed. The room, with its oppressive shadows, that lingering heaviness and heat, unsettled her. She was beginning to understand why her great-uncle had slept with a loaded pistol within grasping range. For such a large bedroom in such a large house, she felt curiously vulnerable. There was none of the coziness here she had known in her parents' too-small home.

Marianne flipped idly through a book—Pope's translation of the Iliad—but Hector's dismemberment made her queasy and she struggled to make sense of the couplets. Her eyes returned again and again to the portrait. Finally, Marianne knew she wasn't going to get any more sleep if the portrait remained, so she clambered out of bed and, after dragging a chair to the wall and standing on it, managed to detach the picture from the wall, revealing a patch of wall and a collection of dust that left Marianne coughing.

This done, Marianne got back into bed, tucking the sheets thick around her, to give herself the illusion of security.

But now, rather than heat, Marianne began to feel a spreading cold. Her toes curled, almost involuntarily, and she felt the book grow heavy in her hands. She was not alone.

With a suddenness like a shot, the candle blew out, and Marianne felt her throat go numb, as if a burst of cold had passed over her.

"Is someone there?" she asked.

And she was not left waiting for an answer long.

Marianne had no idea what she had gotten herself into.

After a largely sleepless night punctuated by odd sounds and strange chills that spread eerily across the bedroom, Marianne had slipped into a doze from which she awoke at midday, heart pounding and fists clenched.

But the room was, at midday, totally devoid of the things that had frightened her the night before. Sun had spread across the floor, and the portrait of Mrs. Babbage, which Marianne had removed from the wall, sat harmlessly against the floor.

Marianne washed her face free of the sweat that had stained it and rang for Mrs. Grubert, with an ancient bell that she imagined her great-uncle had used during his last illness.

Mrs. Grubert appeared eventually. "Up at last," she said to Marianne. "You'll be wanting something to eat?"

"I want to know——" Marianne stopped herself. She had wanted to say, "I want to know why this room is haunted." But staring at Mrs. Grubert's solid, sensible face, Marianne couldn't bring herself to say something so fanciful. Instead, she said, with what she hoped was a good approximation of carelessness, "I want to know the history of the house. You spoke yesterday briefly of its history as a priory. But I want to know how Uncle acquired it. It's my house now. I have a right to know about it."

"Yes, ma'am," Mrs. Grubert said. "Your uncle was a great lover of history himself. I can show you the books he wrote on the subject."

Marianne nodded.

"Breakfast?" Mrs. Grubert nodded.

"Yes," Marianne said. Even in her deepest distress, her appetite was not likely to desert her. "Eggs, please, and porridge."

"I will bring it to the study," Mrs. Grubert said.

After eating, Marianne felt herself slowly returning to normal. Maybe last night's experiences hadn't been supernatural. Maybe, instead, she had been overcome with nerves at being in a strange place. Maybe she should summon a clergyman to the house. She wished she could send for her father, but he was in Dair, and Marianne needed to know the locals anyway. Mrs. Grubert would know that sort of thing.

But still, Marianne was a habitual reader and was curious to see what her great-uncle had written on the history of his house. Perhaps that would shed some light on the strangeness of the bedroom, the way it had seemed to grow so cold, unnaturally cold, with the fading light—

Marianne shook her head. She needed to rein in her imagination. She tried to picture her sister Soph, who would have laughed at Marianne's fears. Soph was a relentless pragmatist, even at nine. No ghost could have haunted her.

And so Marianne set to reading. The books Mrs. Grubert had set out were mostly written by people other than her great-uncle, but one volume was written by him. She recognized vaguely his spidery scrawl. But after several hours' worth of reading, Marianne had learned only that the house was even older than she had initially been told, and that her Uncle lacked the virtue of brevity. But there was nothing that hinted at any supernatural activity, no ghost stories, and nothing, even in her uncle's writing, about his late wife.

Marianne was frustratedly arranging books back on the shelves when a thought occurred to her: there was a volume on the shelves labeled Prayer Book.

But had her great-uncle not been vehemently against organized religion? Why would he have a prayer book?

Taking it in her hands, Marianne began flipping through it. The handwriting was different than her uncle's—it was the handwriting of a woman. Marianne recognized in it a certain delicacy, distinct from her Uncle's thin, decisive strokes.

Could it be—

Marianne turned back to the first page, and her guess was proven correct:

Property of Mrs. Lavinia Babbage

The door began to open and Marianne instinctively shoved the book between folds of her skirt.

"Were those volumes helpful, ma'am?" Mrs. Grubert asked.

"Yes, very much," Marianne said. "Very helpful."

Mrs. Grubert nodded, but she lingered in the doorway. "Is there anything you need?"

"Yes, more candles in my room," Marianne said. "I plan on doing more reading tonight."

"You be careful with that late-night reading," Mrs. Grubert said. "You'll burn yourself in your bed, if you're not wise."

"I'll be careful," Marianne said.

Mrs. Grubert left, and Marianne slipped the book into her rather large pockets.

She had scarcely begun debating the merits of reading the book now or later, wondering at her aversion to being seen by Mrs. Grubert with the book, when the door reopened. This time Mrs. Grubert appeared perplexed.

"Yes?" Marianne said.

"There are three young gentlemen here to see you," Mrs. Grubert said.

"I know no young gentlemen," Marianne said.

"They say they won't leave without seeing you," Mrs. Grubert said.

"Did they say what they want?" Marianne said.

Mrs. Grubert said, "No, but they looked rather . . ."

"What?" Marianne said.

"Bedraggled," Mrs. Grubert said.

Marianne nodded. "Where's Hamish?"

"Out back, I imagine," Mrs. Grubert said.

"Fetch him," Marianne said, "in case something should happen."

She rose and went downstairs, trying not to think that she was about to be beaten and robbed by three strange men.

At the foot of the stairs, she heard them before she saw them, and the voices struck her as familiar somehow, but she couldn't place them.

"Hush," one was saying. "Just let me do the talking."

Marianne rounded the corner, passing into the Great Hall. It was late enough that Hamish had already started a fire and Marianne found herself staring at the silhouettes of three young men before turning to see them in actuality.

"I am Marianne Keyes," she said. "Who are you?"

One toward the left stepped forward. "My name is Richard, ma'am, and I'm so sorry to bother you, but you see, we've been set upon by highwaymen and forced to abandon our belongings." He managed a pained but simple smile. Marianne supposed some women might have called him handsome. He had a drooping mustache, which was rather distracting.

"Highwaymen?" Marianne said. "In this part of the country?"

"We were shocked too," another one said. "My name is Arthur, ma'am."

"I'm George," said the third.

They were all in varying states of dishabille, and looked none too clean either, but there was an air about them, a sense of their being gentlemen. She could have sworn she knew their voices . . . Were they friends of her father's? No, they were far too young. But how else could she have heard them before?

"And what do you require from me?" Marianne said.

"We beg your understanding, ma'am," the first—Richard—said. "It's just, we find ourselves in need of a place to stay, for just the night, and perhaps a meal or two. We need to send a letter to London to secure funds. Then we'll be on our way and continue our trip."

"Where were you going?" Marianne asked, something still bothering her about this. She knew she'd heard their voices before . . .

"To the Lake District," Richard said. "I craved an escape from city life. One can only go to the opera so many times before it begins to pale in comparison to the natural grandeur of nature."

Marianne nodded. She wished her father were there, to tell her what to say. But she was in charge, and she had to make the call.

And then it hit her.

"Is your eyesight very bad?" she asked the third one—George.

"Um, a bit bad, yes," he said, seeming startled.

"Oh, he's practically blind without his glasses," Arthur said, smiling.

And then Marianne knew. These were the—gentlemen seemed like too generous a description—not-so-gentle men she had overheard insulting her at the opera. What they were doing here she did not know (she couldn't believe their story), and she did not care.

"No, I don't think you can stay," Marianne said.

Richard's smile faded abruptly. "What?" he said.

"No, I'm afraid it just wouldn't be appropriate," Marianne said. "You'll have to leave."

"But—" Richard started.

"No, it just wouldn't do," Marianne said. "Young woman, three strange men, what would the neighbors say?"

"You have no neighbors," George said.

"But if I did, what would they say?" Marianne said. "They'd probably call me a plain, unsightly creature."

"What?" Richard said.

"The door is that way," Marianne said, pointing helpfully toward the exit.

Richard and the others stared at her for a while. "Could we at least have something to drink?"

"There's a well out back," Marianne said. "Hamish will be out there. I've never actually seen or met him, but I'm sure he'll be helpful to you. Goodbye."

And with that, she disappeared upstairs, not wanting to see them leave. Besides, she had reading to do. The prayer book of Mrs. Lavinia Babbage wasn't going to reveal its secrets without her.

Chapter Four: A New Flame

As soon as the door closed on them and they'd managed to walk a few steps outside, Arthur hissed, "What just happened?"

"I don't know," Richard said. "She was buying it, at first."

"Something happened," Arthur said.

"Was it my glasses?" George said. "After I mentioned my glasses, she got upset."

"Why would she be upset about your glasses?" Arthur said.

"I don't know," George said. "What are we going to do?"

Richard's mind raced. He had assumed that a young woman all alone would be all too eager to be joined by three young men. He had no plan for her disinterest. But he couldn't admit that to Arthur and George.

"We'll wait right here," Richard said. "Well, not right here—we'll hide out in the woods."

"Wait for what?" Arthur said.

"She'll change her mind," Richard said. "Although we may have to be more inventive. I don't think she bought the robbery story. Maybe I can pretend I have a deadly disease. Women love nursing men back to health."

"Wait in the woods?" George said. "But I'm hungry."

"Do you have a better idea?" Richard said.

"No," George admitted.

"Then we're waiting," Richard said.

"Waiting for what, exactly?" Arthur said.

"I don't know," Richard said. "Just waiting—until tomorrow morning. If all else fails, we can say we were set upon again."

"By whom? Other highwaymen?" Arthur said.

"How many highwaymen can we reasonably claim to have been robbed by?" George said.

"I don't know," Richard hissed. "I need time to think." He pulled his coat around himself, feeling very inconvenienced.

"I bet it'll be freezing," Arthur moaned, though settling obediently against a tree trunk.

"Hush," Richard said. "We don't need that groundskeeper finding us. Besides, we've been in worse scrapes. Remember that time we got kicked out of the villa in Italy?"

"Do I?" Arthur said. "That was the longest night of my life."

"Longer than this one's going to be?" George muttered.

And Richard settled in for a long, long night.

Richard was a light sleeper, when his sleep wasn't deepened by alcohol.

So when he woke to find the moon still high in the sky, he wasn't surprised. He felt more surprised that he'd managed to sleep at all. George and Arthur had curled up against their respective trees. George's glasses had slipped halfway down his face. Arthur was drooling on his shirtfront.

Richard sighed and began to adjust his posture, in a futile attempt to get comfortable. (Dammit, it was cold. He wished they could have managed a fire.)

Perhaps it was then, at the thought of fire, that he thought he saw it. Just the glimmer, in the corner of his eye. Something orange.

Rising to his feet, which provoked a lot of creaking in his joints (Richard was no longer eighteen years old and could not spend a night on the ground without consequences), Richard went in search of what his cold hands made him hope was fire. Maybe there was another band of three young noblemen out in the woods. Maybe they would share their supplies, if they had any.

Richard sighed. It seemed like his talent consisted mostly of lying to himself these days.

He tread heavily through the woods, unable to manage stealth when his joints were frozen and stiff. He followed the glimmers of orange and was surprised to find himself being led to the edge of the woods. He would have thought anyone starting a fire on private property would have wanted to hide in the forest, as they had done.

It was when he neared the edge of the forest, coming dangerously close to the drive of the estate, that he began to smell the smoke. How big was this fire? Perhaps, he began to wonder uneasily, a band of highwaymen really had descended on the countryside and decided to burn it down.

Then he saw the house and, on the second story, a bright square of flame framed within a window. Smoke was pouring from the room.

"George! Arthur!" Richard screamed, in a voice that definitely did not sound like a little girl's. "Fire! Fire!" He could hear Arthur and George blundering through the woods. "Fire!" Richard screamed one more, just for good measure, and barreled toward the house, as he planned to do—something.

He flung open the front door, which wasn't even locked (of course it wasn't), and found himself being stared at by a dozen dead animals on the walls. He felt Arthur behind him and George, panting heavily. "Where's the fire?" Arthur yelled.

"Smoke! There!" George shouted, pointing at the doorway toward the east, underneath which smoke was, indeed, pouring.

They took off toward the smoke and ran into a corridor and then, up stairs. The smoke was very thick and Richard wasn't sure if he was the one coughing or Arthur or George. He knew he could barely breathe, and he shoved his cravat into his mouth, as if that would help.

"Come on!" he shouted. They took off down a hallway and Arthur began flinging open doors.

They arrived, then, at the end of the hall and Richard flung open the last door, revealing a wreath of flame.

Arthur swore and George began coughing profusely.

"We need to beat it down!" George said and took off his coat and began beating at the flames, which responded by growing larger. But it bought Richard enough time to dart through the doorway into a room filled with smoke. And in the center of the room, in the middle of a bed now aflame, lay the disagreeable Marianne Keyes, eyes closed, mouth shut. Was she dead?

Richard had no time for delicacy. He seized her torso, dragging her body from the bed. A piece of flaming bed curtain hit his cheek, and he screamed in pain, then Arthur was beside him, tugging Marianne out of the room.

George had managed through strenuous exertion to batter the flames at the doorway down temporarily, and Richard and Arthur managed to drag Marianne through, then down the stairs and, somehow, back through the Great Hall and then outside, where she was laid on the ground. She was unmoving.

"Is she dead?" George asked.

Richard couldn't speak, he was coughing so badly. Only doubled over could he manage to say, "Check her pulse."

Arthur grabbed her wrist. "She's alive."

"Why is she not breathing?" George said.

"Where did they say the water was?" Richard said.

"In the back," Arthur said.

Richard took off as fast as he could, which was a fast hobble with his current lungfuls of smoke, and began searching the overgrown grounds for the well. When he found it, he filled a bucket and hobbled back to Marianne, where he unceremoniously dumped water on her prostrate form.

She sat up, gasping.

She took in the three men, the ashy plumes emitting from the open window and managed, after coughing, "What's happened?"

"Someone just tried to kill you," Richard said.

Chapter Five: Mystery at Rothmore

Marianne puzzled over the events of the previous night as she turned over porridge with her spoon.

After being awakened by Richard, she had witnessed a startled Hamish—a man, it turned out, roughly her father's age and with a beard the length of his belt—sprint out of the groundkeeper's cottage and begin dumping water onto the room that had so recently been hers. The others, George and Arthur, had assisted.

By sunrise, the fire had dissipated, leaving the charred remains of a room and Marianne, more shaken than she wanted to show. But how could she not show it? Richard had said what they were all thinking—someone had tried to kill her.

"Maybe," she had said, when the flames were extinguished, and they were all sitting outside on the drive, dead tired and coughing, "it was just an accident." She had been using a candle to read when she fell asleep.

"Did you blow out the candle?" Richard asked.

"Of course," she said.

"Unless candles can now spontaneously reignite, then that doesn't explain this," Richard said. His mustache looked sooty.

"Is there anyone who might want to harm you?" George had asked.

"No," Marianne said. "I mean, no one other than—" She had stopped short.

"What, other than us?" Arthur said.

"Yes," Marianne said. "You didn't look pleased when I sent you away."

"Why would we try to kill you and then rescue you?" George said.

They had a point there.

"Maybe you were trying to trick me," Marianne said. "And get me to trust you."

"Do we look like we're capable of that kind of a plan?" Arthur said.

"No," Marianne said.

Arthur's dark hair was swept handsomely against his sooty forehead. Aside from his unkempt mustache, Richard also appeared surprisingly collected. One would think he battled fires on a nightly basis. George was occupied cleaning his glasses, his large frame hunched slightly, but he had the stolid self-possession that some wealthy people never lose, even after running out of a fire. Marianne was a little irritated that the three gentlemen managed to appear suave even when dirty and smoky. She felt like a charbroiled mouse. She was fairly certain her hair was smoking. Then she felt irritated with herself for thinking of something so vain as appearances at a time like this. She just wasn't used to being around young men, that was all. She hoped she wouldn't have to get used to it.

George replaced his glasses, squinting at the house behind them. "Then either this is some freak phenomenon, or—"

"It was attempted murder," Richard said.

"Are you sure you didn't forget to blow out your candle?" George asked.

Marianne said, with more certainty than she felt, "I know it was out. The room was completely dark when I fell asleep. Except—"

"Except what?" Richard asked sharply.

"Nothing," Marianne said. She was reluctant to bring up strange chills in front of three men who had mocked her at an opera. She didn't want them to mock her yet again for superstition.

Marianne changed the subject abruptly. "But what would someone hope to gain through my death?"

"You have money, don't you?" Richard said.

"Not here," Marianne said. "It's in the care of my solicitor."

"Maybe it was revenge," Arthur said. "Are you sure you haven't angered anyone?"

"No one that I know of," Marianne said, on the verge of tears. She fought to keep her eyes dry, though. She didn't want to cry in front of anyone, let alone these men.

They left off talking then, when Hamish returned to tell them they could now go inside. The house didn't appear structurally damaged, but Marianne's bedroom was unusable.

It wasn't until later, after Marianne had apprised a startled Mrs. Grubert of the night's events, after Richard, George, and Arthur had been invited to stay for breakfast, that it occurred to Marianne—

"It's gone," she said.

Richard, George, and Arthur looked up from their plates. George had been inhaling kippers as Richard and Arthur devoured piles of toast. "What's gone?" George said through a mouthful of kipper.

"The book," Marianne said.

"You can get another book," Richard said.

"No, it was—" Marianne stopped speaking as Mrs. Grubert entered to dole out fresh batches of toast. It was only when she left that Marianne whispered across the table, "A book about my late great-aunt. I wasn't supposed to have it in the first place. It must have been destroyed in the fire."

"What sort of a book was it?" Richard said sharply.

"A diary," Marianne said.

"Was there something bad in it?" Richard said. "Something someone wouldn't want you to see?"

"No, it was just about her daily life," Marianne said. "Except—"

"Except what?" Richard said. George and Arthur had stopped eating and were looking at her expectantly.

Marianne pushed aside her porridge. "I don't know. I mean, it sounds like lunacy when I really think about it."

"About what?" Richard pressed. His mustache still looked sooty.

"She was writing a lot about feeling sick," Marianne said. "I think she might have been…" She struggled to think of the right word. "She might have been with child."

"Oh," Richard said. "And that's surprising because…"

"Because she had no child," Marianne said. "She died before she could. Or if she was with child, she died before anything came of it."

"Why would someone not want you reading about that?" George said. "It seems harmless enough." To maintain his large—not obese but rather solid—frame, he had piled a great deal of eggs on his plate and was attacking them with a gentlemanly vengeance. Marianne admired his dedication to food. It was something that they shared.

"I don't know," Marianne said.

"You think that's why the fire was started?" George said after swallowing a substantial quantity of egg. "To get rid of the book?"

"Or you," Richard said, looking at Marianne. "It's not safe here," he said to her. "You'll have to leave."

"But I can't!" Marianne said. "I have to stay, or I don't get my inheritance!"

"Ah," Richard said, leaning back in his chair. "Maybe someone's trying to drive you out, then. To keep you from the money?"

"But no one else has any claim to the money," Marianne said.

"That you know of," Arthur said.

Marianne was troubled by this. What if there was more to her great-uncle's will than she knew? What if someone tried to hurt her again?

Realizing that her hands were shaking, Marianne quickly put them beneath the table. "Please, you all have to stay. I know it's terribly dangerous, but I can't leave without sacrificing my inheritance. If you can stay, I'd be so grateful."

Richard, George, and Arthur exchanged glances. "If only to preserve the safety of a lady," Richard said magnanimously.

"But why did you try to get rid of us yesterday?" George said.

Marianne lied easily: "Because it would have been indecent for you to stay. And I didn't know someone was trying to kill me."

Marianne was far from convinced that these three men were the key to her safety. For all she knew, they were the ones who had started the fire. But she didn't think so. After all, it was like they had said. Why would they try to kill her, only to then rescue her? It didn't make any sense. But she had an unsettling suspicion that they were wrapped up in all this. But she didn't know how.

None of it made any sense. Instinctively, when in search of sense, Marianne sought out books, and so Marianne found herself in her great-uncle's library, pacing the floor.

She was strongly tempted to flee to Dair, to explain to her parents what had happened. They wouldn't chastise her for leaving a place she had found to be dangerous, even if there were ten thousand pounds at stake.

But no—Marianne couldn't just leave. She couldn't forfeit what was rightfully hers. Her mother always used to say Marianne's greatest vice was hard-headed stubbornness. But couldn't that also be a good thing, something that would, in a pinch, substitute for courage?

She should, perhaps, have seen the three men away. It would have simplified things. But maybe that's what would deter the would-be arsonist. Maybe complicating things would be better for her.

Except—what if she were endangering the men? What if they were now about to be burned to death in their beds? She didn't care much for them, but she also didn't want them to die.

Marianne suspected that Mrs. Grubert knew more than she admitted. But Mrs. Grubert wouldn't speak to her. Marianne had tried asking about Lavinia Babbage, about the fire, only to get nothing in return.

Marianne stopped pacing. Her heart was racing in her chest, and she lay on the floor, desperate for some semblance of stability. "What is going to happen to me?" she wondered aloud.

She hadn't forgotten, either, that these were the three men who had insulted her at the opera. They weren't nice people, of that she was sure. They were staying for some ulterior motive all their own. But they had saved her life. She didn't want them here, but she needed them, and they had agreed to stay.

Finding herself unsure what else to do, Marianne wrote a letter to her friend Madelyn, by care of Madelyn's aunt in London, including every detail of the fire and her strange rescue, along with the disappearance of Lavinia Babbage's prayer book and what Arthur had said about something wanting to drive Marianne from Rothmore and, consequently, her inheritance. After she'd finished writing, Marianne's wrist was very sore, and she needed to post a letter in the village. She didn't trust Mrs. Grubert to do it.

Gathering her things, Marianne prepared to walk to the village. She was descending downstairs when she ran into Richard, who had managed to return his mustache to a decent color. His clothes, however, still smelled strongly of smoke.

"Miss Keyes," he said. "Where are you off to?"

None of your business, she wanted to say. But that wasn't a very nice thing to say to the man who had saved her life. "The village," she said. "To post a letter. You smell of soot."

"Do I?" Richard said. "I hadn't noticed. Why don't you wait for us? We'll be happy to accompany you."

"I'm not in need of an armed guard during daylight, I hope," Marianne said. "Although your chivalry is duly noted."

She proceeded a few steps, but he managed to run in front of her. "If you're not in need of a guard, what about friends?" he said.

"I prefer friends of the female variety," Marianne said.

"In their absence, would you accept a man?" Richard said.

She could see she wasn't getting rid of him.

"All right," Marianne said, defeated.

And so Richard and Marianne set off for the village, accompanied by George and Arthur who, after exchanging knowing glances with Richard, seemed content to stray a few paces behind.

Within the first half hour, Richard had to admit defeat. He left Marianne to poke at some mushrooms and scurried to where George and Arthur were standing, pretending to admire an oak. "What are you doing?" Arthur hissed the moment Richard was within earshot. "Lay on the charm!"

"I'm trying!" Richard said. "But nothing's working."

"You told her you had written that poem about her?" Arthur said.

"I started to, but then she started off on Pope's philosophy of God," Richard said.

"What about the thing where you tell her about a time a woman broke your heart and left you shattered and broken, and you need for her to pick up the pieces?" Arthur said.

"I started to, but she kept wanting to talk about the fire," Richard said. "It's damned hard to make love to a woman when she keeps going on about being almost murdered."

"She's bound to be a bit distracted today," George said. "You've just got to keep trying. We need that money!

"Come on, Richard," Arthur said, "get in there! Charm this heifer!"

"Fine," Richard said. "But it's a lot harder than it looks." He sighed and smoothed his mustache. Arthur was right. He needed to be charming. And he knew he could be. Many women had told him he was. They couldn't all have been lying.

Pasting on a smile, Richard approached Marianne, who was kneeling beside a mushroom. She sighed and rose. "Definitely poisonous," she said.

"What?" Richard said.

"Those mushrooms. One bite and we'd be dead," Marianne said. "Goodness, there are rather a lot of ways to die, aren't there?"

Richard felt the conversation slipping away from him. "Maybe," he said, "what you need is to contemplate less morbid topics. You've talked of nothing but death all day. You should be thinking about life and your future."

"You're right," Marianne said. "I need to see about restoring the bedroom in Rothmore. Perhaps I can find someone in the village to do it."

"I meant, your personal future," Richard said.

"What about it?" Marianne said.

"Well, you're a young woman," Richard said.

"That's debatable," Marianne said.

"Wait, what?" Richard said.

"Am I young?" Marianne said. "I'm twenty-four. I can't exactly be called young anymore. I'm properly grown up, surely."

"All the more reason for you to think about your future," Richard said. "Have you ever considered marriage?"

"No," Marianne said. "Have you?"

"I-I could be persuaded," Richard said, preparing to resume his narrative about his heartbroken past and needing his heart put back together again.

"You should never marry," Marianne said.

"What, why?" Richard said.

"You're deeply critical of women you can't control," Marianne said. "I sense it. I suspect you had a strained relationship with your mother."

"I did not!" Richard said. "My father, on the other hand—"

"It typically manifests that way," Marianne said, sighing.

"Manifests?" Richard said.

"Resentment toward the mother often gets disguised as resentment toward the father," Marianne said. "You resent the father for distancing you from the mother, when in fact, you've actually distanced yourself from your mother. The father is just a distraction."

"What? I haven't distanced myself from anyone," Richard said.

"If you say so," Marianne said. "But Rousseau would disagree. At least, I think it was Rousseau. Did he say that or someone else?"

"You've read Rousseau?" Richard said.

"Obviously not well enough," Marianne said. "My father always said the man's personal morals didn't exactly recommend him as a tutor to the young."

Richard turned to see George and Arthur. "Get on with it!" Arthur mouthed at him.

"Marianne," Richard said, "has anyone ever told you you're very pretty?"

"In this dress?" Marianne said. "But it's blue. Pair it with a clergyman, and I'd be a real sight."

"What?" Richard said. "What's that got to do with anything?"

"Nothing," Marianne sighed.

They walked the rest of the way to the village in relative silence.

Richard wasn't sure how to proceed. He knew he needed new clothes, but he had no money, so he and George and Arthur, rather than be reduced to follow Marianne around on her shopping, chose instead to linger at the edge of town while Marianne disappeared into a haberdashery.

"What are you doing?" Arthur said. "Were you talking about Rousseau?"

"She caught me off guard," Richard said. "I'll do better."

"You'll need to work fast," George said. "We're running out of money."

"Running out? We are out," Arthur said. "You must have gotten some advantage by rescuing her last night. Use that."

"How?" Richard said. "The woman is impregnable."

"I don't know," Arthur said. "Ask her if she's still scared for her safety or something. Women love to talk about feeling scared."

Richard nodded. This was true. He had often said that the best time to propose (which he had done several times) was during a thunderstorm. "Nature's excitement inspired other kinds of excitement," he said.

"Did Rousseau say that?" Arthur said.

"Not everything can be attributed to Rousseau," George said.

"No, I suppose not," Arthur said.

"I mean, this whole situation has been handed to you on a silver platter," Arthur said. "You couldn't have planned it better—a young heiress in mortal danger, three dashing young gentlemen saving her, an inheritance in the balance. It's all very novel."

"Speaking of," George said, cleaning his spectacles on the edge of his coat, "did you plan it?"

"What?" Richard said.

"Did you start the fire?" George said.

"I didn't start the fire," Richard said. "I want money, but preferably without murder being involved."

Arthur appeared visibly relieved. George appeared almost…unimpressed.

"What, you thought I had started it?" Richard said.

"The thought crossed my mind," George said. "I would have applauded the initiative."

Richard swore. "How would I have gotten into the house, started the fire, then had time to run back, shout for you to get up, then run back into the house?"

"That thought also crossed my mind," George said.

"Now that we've established that I am not a murderer," Richard said, "Can I get back to being charming?"

"Apparently not. You're not doing a very good job thus far," George said.

"A little more encouragement, George, would be welcome," Richard said.

Arthur slapped Richard on the back. "Get in there, Richard. Make us some money."

Richard tried. He genuinely tried. He tried during their walk back to Rothmore, all during lunch (and dinner), and then in the evening. But it wasn't easy. For one thing, Marianne kept disappearing and reappearing, looking pale and secretive. But then when he asked her what was wrong, she kept saying, "Nothing, nothing." For another, she kept cutting him off whenever he tried to say something even mildly flirtatious. To add to the difficulty, even after they had secured Marianne's permission to spend the night in the house, the housekeeper, Mrs. Grubert made it very clear she did not approve of the situation and kept popping in on Richard and staring at him in a way that made him wonder if his trousers were open. (They weren't.) It was like she was trying to murder him with her eyes.

Compounding this difficulty was simply the fact that Marianne didn't particularly attract Richard. Granted, he had known that this would be the situation. One did not marry an heiress for her beauty. But despite his obsessive standards for women's comeliness, Richard was enough of an artist that he could usually find something about a woman that he admired. But with Marianne, it was hard. She just wasn't a sophisticated looking woman. She looked—well, like a woman who had lived in a small village her whole life and stumbled into an inheritance. She even lacked that pleasant personality rural women sometimes had, a sort of unvarnished vigor and bright enjoyment of life that he liked. No, she was none of those things. Which made it very hard for him to keep relentlessly flirting, especially when Marianne seemed determined to ignore him.

It wasn't until nightfall, when Richard was genuinely worn out with trying to start a conversation with this woman, that she came to him.

Chapter Six: The Attic

Madelyn had, when in Dair, usually come by the house in the afternoon, and, in the rare event Mrs. Keyes had run out of chores to give her daughters—she was always hard at work and so assumed everyone else should be too—Madelyn and Marianne would run into the woods. Madelyn had a gift for telling scary stories. She knew about the myths of Singapore, the strange monsters of Ireland, and she also had ways of getting the latest novels. And Marianne, herself equipped with quite the imagination (a result of reading too many novels, her father would have said), enjoyed the flourishes Madelyn gave even the most absurd stories of hauntings, ghosts, and the like.

Marianne remembered specifically how Madelyn had, through machinations only young women are capable of, acquired The Castle of Otranto, which she and Marianne read breathlessly, beginning to end, in two afternoons.

Sitting in a quickly darkening copse, Marianne had set down the book, eyes wide, and said, "Do you think people are really as evil as Manfred, though? I mean, to divorce his wife and marry his daughter-in-law, then to kill Matilda! It's so awful!"

Madelyn sighed with that world weariness she, at the ripe age of nineteen, could manage so well. "When people are rich, there's no one to dissuade them from their worst instincts."

"Have you met many rich people?" Marianne had asked.

"No," Madelyn had to admit, "but it's a matter of logic. Morals have to be enforced by social bounds and laws. When someone has wealth, they are unaffected by social bounds and laws. So their actions are never checked."

"I suppose not," Marianne had said. "But… But wouldn't it be wonderful, to have so much money, no one could tell you what to do, ever again?"

"Then you'd turn into Manfred," Madelyn had said, "and go around stabbing people and stealing kingdoms."

"But—" Marianne struggled to articulate a feeling she was slightly ashamed of. "But what if wealth doesn't make someone good or bad? What if it just exaggerates and enables our natural tendencies? So if we want to do good, wealth enables us to do more good. If we want to do evil, wealth enables that too. Does wealth have to be innately corrupting?"

Madelyn had considered for a while and the setting sun had fallen on the leaves in such a way that the shadows had dappled her face, obscuring her eyes in shadow. "That's the thing, though. Wealth enables us to attain our desires. And everyone thinks they desire good things. But what if we don't acknowledge what our desires really are until we're in a position to attain them? What if we think we want good things, until we're in a position to attain bad things, then we discover that we are . . ."

"Villains," Marianne said.

"Well, yes," Madelyn said. "But we never know, until we have the money to realize what it is we really want."

"But—" Marianne had been interrupted by a call from Madelyn's brother (younger and very annoying in the way that all younger brothers delight in being) to return home. And the conversation had ended.

But five years later, and in the dimly lit halls of Rothmore, Marianne had cause to reflect on what Madelyn had said. Did wealth illuminate dark desires lurking in the heart of even the most seemingly innocent person? Was she, Marianne, implicated in some way that she couldn't identify, in some strange goings-on? Why else would someone want to do her harm?

She was determined to find out.

But certain of her guests were not making it easy.

Marianne tried to escape Richard most of the day. He may have saved her life, but he was very awkward to be around. He kept trying to talk to her about strange things, which she did not want to talk about, especially to the man who had called her a plain creature at the opera. But whenever she was tempted to rescind her invitation to stay the night, she only needed to remind herself that she didn't really want to be alone in the house again. Not after what had happened the previous night.

Her lungs still didn't feel normal, and while climbing the stairs, she began wheezing. She was very glad none of the young men saw that. The last thing she needed was them catching her in a moment of vulnerability.

Mrs. Grubert kept trying to get Marianne to sit down, but Marianne, who did not know if she could trust Mrs. Grubert, refused, instead pleading a headache and saying she wanted to lie down. This wasn't altogether a lie, but Marianne spent only a fraction of the day actually lying down. It had occurred to her, when returning home from the village—a very charming place called Bickersmore—that the house seemed different from the outside than it did the inside.

Richard had been talking at her, something about sublimity?

"—that strange quality that Pope calls 'awful beauty putting on all its arms'."

"Mr. Lowell," Marianne interrupted. "Do you think the house looks strange?"

Richard had stared at Rothmore. George and Arthur had lingered behind, pretending to discuss with Hamish some particulars of the property. "Strange how?"

"Strange, like it should be shorter than it is," Marianne said. "There's only two stories, isn't there? But there's a third row of windows, up there." She pointed.

"Yes, very strange," Richard said. "Now about beauty—"

"Very strange," Marianne said. "Well, goodbye. I have to attend to my toilette." And she had left him to talk poetry by himself.

But Marianne had not attended to her toilette. She had, instead, gone to the second story and, after ascertaining that Mrs. Grubert was safely downstairs, began looking at the ceilings, to see if there was any hint of an entrance to an attic.

The afternoon had passed mostly without discovery. None of the ceilings seemed to hint at anything like a ladder or even a place where a ladder may once have been.

It wasn't until late, after she had eaten dinner, evaded Mrs. Grubert yet again, and managed to slip back upstairs, that Marianne found what she was looking for: in a closet, at the very backmost corner of what must once have been a monk's cell during Rothmore's time as a priory, right above an ancient chamber pot emitting an unpleasant smell, a section of wood that looked different from the surrounding wood. It was, if she was not mistaken, a sort of access door to the attic. But it hadn't been used recently, judging from the thick layer of dust in the room.

Marianne tried to open the door to the attic, but it was too high for her. She had to put that endeavor on hold while she sought out a stool, which required going downstairs, lying to Mrs. Grubert about her occupations, then returning upstairs with the stool smuggled beneath her skirts.

She was walking upstairs when she bumped into Mr. Lowell, who was insisting she call him Richard, although that seemed rather informal, especially since she had vowed to hate him eternally. But he had saved her life, so maybe Richard was a good compromise?

"Off to bed?" Mr. Lowell/Richard had asked.

"Indeed," Marianne said. She tried to squeeze past him on the stairs, but he caught her arm.

"Will you permit me to address you tomorrow?" he asked. "In private."

"I think I'll be busy," Marianne said.

"Oh," he said. "Perhaps the next day?"

"I'll be busy then too," Marianne said.

She tried to squeeze past him again, but it was in the forceful maneuvering of her skirts past his legs that the stool slipped from where she had positioned it so carefully, and it fell heavily to the floor.

"What have you got under there?" Richard asked, staring at her skirts.

"Nothing, it's just a…a stool," Marianne said.

Richard's eyebrows went to his hairline. "Why are you carrying a stool under your skirt?" Except this question didn't seem like anything else he'd said. It felt—honest. Genuine. He really wanted to know.

Marianne wouldn't have told him. Except—she thought she heard Mrs. Grubert rounding the corner, keys jangling. And so she whispered, "I don't want Mrs. Grubert to see."

"Are you doing something secretive?" Richard said.

"I'm trying to get into the attic, and I don't know if she'd want me to," Marianne said.

"There is an attic?" Richard said.

The keys jangled again, signalling Mrs. Grubert's approach, and Marianne darted up the stairs, stool in hand, followed closely behind by Richard.

When they arrived at the back closet, Richard watched as Marianne quickly stowed the stool, then ran to the guest room that had been newly designated hers.

Mrs. Grubert asked if Marianne needed anything. Marianne said she didn't.

"Are the gentlemen settled in for the night?" Marianne asked.

"Aye, although if you ask me, it's all highly irregular," Mrs. Grubert answered.

"Yes, I know," Marianne said. "But one can never be too careful when living alone. It's always good to have guests. Besides, I wouldn't want to be thought of as inhospitable. That's hardly a good reputation to be cultivating, is it?" Richard thought Marianne's voice sounded so—in control. It was hard to believe she was only twenty-four years old. She sounded like a competent middle-aged woman.

"No, ma'am," Mrs. Grubert said.

Then the housekeeper retired downstairs. Richard was wondering if Marianne truly had gone to sleep when Marianne emerged from her room. She slipped past him into a far room, then positioned the stool beneath a section of ceiling. Upon her reappearing, with her rather large eyes and full, still somewhat childish features, that Richard saw how young she really was. So was the voice a performance, that air or competence and distant practicality? Was the strange, youthful enormity of her eyes the real Marianne?

Richard was somewhat surprised that he even cared.

"So?" Richard said, shaking himself out of his train of thought.

"Look," Marianne said. "It's like...like a trapdoor to the attic."

Richard stared at it, but the room was too dark, and he couldn't see what Marianne said was there. "Let me get a light," he said. He fumbled his way out of the room and back with a candle from the study. The illumination of the candle did reveal a certain rectangular section in the ceiling that did look rather like a trapdoor.

"I can't reach it," Marianne said, getting off the stool, on which she had been perched.

"Let me try," Richard said. He had height to his advantage and managed to reach the door, but he couldn't budge it. "It's stuck," he said, sweat beginning to bead on his forehead. The room was very stuffy, and he was pushing very hard against a door that wasn't moving.

"Hold on," he said, returning to the ground. "Let me think. Maybe... Let me get Arthur and George. They can help."

"All right," Marianne said. "But be quiet!" Again, Richard could hear the distant competence in her voice, in that—not aloof, but somewhat cold—way of hers, but also, maybe, some fear? He decided to focus on that. The fear he could understand. The fear was human. The poet in him could respect the sincerity of it.

Richard nodded. And to his credit, he moved downstairs very stealthily. When he got to George and Arthur, who had bedded down in the dining room on two divans, Arthur said, "Don't tell me there's another fire."

"No, just a mysterious trapdoor to an attic," Richard said.

"Count me in," Arthur said, rising sleepily. .

"I'd rather not be in, personally," George said.

"Come on," Richard said. "I can't open it by myself. It's stuck or something."

"Fine," George said with a sigh, putting on his spectacles and following Richard upstairs.

They managed to find the closet and, in it, Marianne, without awakening Mrs. Grubert, little thanks to Arthur, who stubbed his toe on an errant board and whose swearing almost broke the silence.

When they reached her, Marianne had regained the stool and was still shoving at the door, to no avail. She was balancing on two large volumes of Mandeville's Fable of the Bees, and the stool wobbled unsteadily as she exerted herself.

"Hey, that's not safe," Richard said, and, without really thinking about it, grabbed Marianne's waist and set her down on the floor.

After he'd done it, he could feel himself immediately regret it. He had never done that before—just grabbed a woman, even if it was for her own safety, unless he was being amorous or at least flirtatious. And he genuinely hadn't meant to be flirtatious in the moment. His honest curiosity about the trapdoor had been awakened, and he had been thinking about that. But here he was, with ten thousand pounds in the balance, and he had just grabbed a woman unthinkingly.

Maybe because he had touched her last night, when dragging her from the fire, his instincts in this matter were no longer good?

"Sorry," he said.

"It's all right," Marianne said tightly.

If Arthur and George noticed, they said nothing. Arthur had clambered onto the stool and was shoving at the trapdoor. "George, it'll take your strength to move this," Arthur said.

George reluctantly switched places with Arthur and began shoving at the trapdoor. George was a large, squarish man with a surprising amount of strength. And when he shoved the trapdoor, it moved, sending a loud crack resounding through the room.

"Oh, no," Marianne breathed. "Mrs. Grubert will have heard."

But there was no jangle of keys, no matronly inquiry. "I think we're safe," Arthur said.

The trapdoor had swung down and, with it, a ladder.

"Do I dare?" Richard said.

"I have to go up," Marianne said. "It's my house. I need to know what's up there."

"It may not be safe," Richard said.

"Safe? I was nearly killed last night. We're past safe," Marianne said.

"Let me go first," Arthur said, in a show of chivalry.

"No, let me go first," Richard said, seizing Arthur's hand and squeezing. Couldn't Arthur tell that Richard needed to look like the most gallant one there?

"Oh, right," Arthur said. "Go ahead."

But when Richard climbed onto the ladder, he wished Arthur were going first.

He tried one step, then another, then another, moving slowly into the unfamiliar dark.

"Hand up the light," Richard said, and George handed him the candle, which Richard raised above him. He clambered up the steps and onto the floor of the attic. Raising the candle to his eye level, he examined the room. It was large, mostly open space with old furnishings strewn throughout. "Not much up here," he said down to the others.

"I'm coming up," Arthur said, and Richard helped Arthur, then George, and, finally, Marianne, to climb into the attic.

"Careful where you step," Arthur said. "Who knows how solid any of this is."

Richard went first, inching across the expanse of floor.

"You all right, Richard?" George said, sounding worried.

"If I go crashing through the floor, bury me with the poets," Richard said, sweat trickling down the back of his neck.

"Are those your last words?" Arthur said.

"Hopefully not," Richard said. "Give me time to think of something more clever."

He inched his way across the floor, until his foot collided with something large and unforgiving, and he began swearing.

"Don't tell me that's the 'something clever'," Arthur said.

"Are you all right?" Marianne asked.

"No," Richard said. "I mean, yes. I just rammed my foot into this thing." He felt around his foot for the obstacle, and careful not to lose his grip on the candle in his other hand, grabbed a small but stout box.

"What is it?" George said, squinting into the dark.

"Some sort of chest," Richard said. "Give me a minute." He inched his way back toward the group and handed it to Arthur. The four stood around the box. "Can you open it?"

Arthur strained. "It's stuck too," he said.

"The hinges are rusty," Marianne said. "Bring it downstairs—I have something that'll loosen it."

"Just a moment," Richard said. "Let me look around a little more, while we're up here."

He inched his way across the attic.

"Careful!" Arthur said.

There was a sharp intake of breath. "There's a lot of water damage in this section," Richard said. "I don't know how much weight it would take, but I think with one errant step, a man could bust through."

Marianne sighed. "How much would that cost to fix?"

"No telling," George said. "Depends on how extensive the initial leak is."

Marianne shook her head. "I can't think about that now. Let's just worry about the trunk for the moment."

They retreated down the ladder. Marianne disappeared back into her new bedroom, returning with a jar of some substance. She began smearing it on the hinges.

Arthur strained again, and the box clicked as it opened.

"What is that stuff?" Richard said.

"Hair pomade," Marianne said. "My mother used it all the time to unstick things."

Richard had not considered that Marianne had a mother. Well, he had obviously known Marianne had a mother. But he had not specifically pictured her with a mother. Or indeed, any family. The thought made him uncomfortable for some reason, and he shoved it away.

"Hold the candle higher, George," Arthur said, and they crowded around the box.

Inside the box there were several papers. Marianne carefully unfolded some. "They're letters," she said, after a moment's reading. "From my great-uncle to Lavinia!"

"Who's Lavinia?" George whispered.

"My great-aunt," Marianne said. "The one whose journal was burned in the fire. She died in this house."

"Died of what?" Arthur said.

"I don't know," Marianne said. "Maybe these letters say something about it."

They decamped to the study, where they each took a pile of letters.

"This one is just about his undying love for Lavinia," Arthur said, yawning.

"This one says he's in the Alps," George said.

"This one, this one is interesting," Richard said.

"What?" Marianne said.

"Listen to this: 'My dear, the visitations you mentioned in your last letter have disturbed me greatly, more so for your sake than mine. I wish you to spend time away from Rothmore until I have returned. Then, together, we can make the old house a home. For me, no place can be a home, without you.'"

"What does he mean, 'visitations'?" Arthur said.

"Unwanted guests?" Richard said.

"Spiritual occurrences?" George said. "Marianne, have you had any spiritual occurrences?"

Marianne was silent.

"Well?" Richard said.

"Perhaps," Marianne said. She told them about her first night at Rothmore and the portrait of Lavinia that had kept her awake, along with the strange chill. "But I was just nervous to be away from home for the first time," Marianne said. "I probably imagined it."

"You didn't imagine the fire last night," Arthur said.

"No," Marianne conceded. "I did not imagine that."

"Is the place haunted, do you think?" Arthur said.

Richard wanted to laugh. "Come on, Arthur, you know better than that. That's all superstitious tripe dredged up by old wives and religious leaders to keep us compliant."

"I guess now would be a good time to mention that my father is a clergyman," Marianne said.

"Forget what I said about the religious leaders, then," Richard said.

"Why?" Marianne said. "If it's something you truly believe."

Richard found himself caught. "I, well, I didn't mean to insult your father particularly," he said. (It still made him uncomfortable to think of Marianne having a family. But why? He wasn't sure.) "I haven't had good experiences with the clergy in general."

"I believe in one tract you call them 'professors of hypocrisy'," Arthur said, not at all helpfully.

"That's a bit harsh," Marianne said. "Do you honestly believe that?"

"I don't…that's not… I consider myself an atheist for a reason, all right?" Richard said.

"An atheist?" Marianne said. "I've never actually met one of those."

"Now you have," Richard said, but he sounded short. Why was he sounding irritated? He needed to be sounding charming, not irritated.

"Straying from Richard's spiritual crisis," George said dryly, "I must again ask, is this estate haunted?"

"Haunted in what way?" Marianne said.

"I mean, is a ghost trying to murder you?" George said.

"How would one tell?" Marianne said.

"We keep reading," Richard said, eager to be off the topic of his atheism.

And so they did. The box, though small, contained enough letters to keep them occupied until well after midnight. It was then, when George and Arthur had fallen asleep, that Marianne said, "I've found something."

Richard looked up from his letter. His candle, burning low, was guttering, and his eyes had strained enough to give him a headache. "What is it?" he said.

"Here," Marianne said, trying to hand him the letter.

"Read it to me," Richard said. It had begun to rain very hard, and the sound against the roof, in addition to the thunder, combined with his headache, made him long for sleep. But if Marianne was awake, that meant an opportunity for wooing.

She took a draught of tea to wet her throat and read: "It says, 'Dearest Lavinia, forgive me for my long delay in returning home. Business has kept me abroad longer than I intended. I wish dearly for our reunion.' He goes on like that for a while. Then he says, 'The history of the house, as you know, has rendered it inhospitable to those in your situation. I beg you to exercise caution.'"

"That's it?" Richard said.

"Yes, but think about it," Marianne said. "Isn't he suggesting she's with child? And that the house is not suitable for someone with child?"

"He could be," Richard admitted. "But what would make a house inhospitable specifically to women…in that situation?"

"I don't know," Marianne said.

Thunder clapped and then followed lightning, which shot the sky through with sudden color, illuminating Richard and Marianne.

Marianne, suddenly aware that Richard was a man, and that she was a woman, began to picture her mother walking in on them. Mrs. Keyes would have been mortified at her daughter being alone with a man at this hour, in a darkened house. Of course, there was nothing romantic happening, but Mrs. Keyes' voice was firm in Marianne's head: This is most improper.

"I should go to bed," Marianne said.

Richard nodded. He was exhausted and in need of rest.

Marianne was at the door to the library when Richard realized he should be more protective: "Are you sure it's safe?" he asked.

"No," Marianne said. "I'll scream if anything happens."

"I'm a light sleeper," Richard said.

And Marianne disappeared upstairs.

Chapter Seven: Blood on the Sheets

Marianne dreamed of the attic and, in it, a monk crouched over a sizable tome.

"Hello," she said to the monk. "I'm dreaming."

The monk looked at her, and Marianne gasped. His eyes were entirely black.

"You should not be here," the monk said. "This is a priory, and women cannot enter."

"It's not a priory anymore," Marianne said. "It's my home. My great-uncle left it to me."

"He should have learned his lesson," the monk said and with that, lunged at Marianne.

Though dreaming, Marianne felt distinctly the sensation of sharp nails across her cheeks, and she struggled. But the monk was very strong, and his height was deceptive. Underneath his habit, he was all sinew, and he hit her very hard, so hard that her head began to ache. And then she was on the ground, and he was on top of her, and then she was flailing, and then she was falling, and falling, and falling . . .

"Marianne! Marianne!" The voice was far away, and then nearer. Whose was it? Her father's? Marianne couldn't recognize it, but she knew it. She knew she knew it.

"Marianne!"

Marianne shot upright, awakened by a sound like wood splintered.

It was still dark, and in the dark, she was puzzled to find herself wet. Was something dripping on her? There was a pounding noise, as if someone were ramming the door repeatedly.

Marianne looked upward and saw, gleaming in the dark, a pair of eyes.

She screamed, louder than she thought it possible to scream, and the door fell inward.

Marianne felt herself being wrenched from her bed, and then she was screaming into a soft surface.

"Marianne, it's all right!" someone said.

"My lord, what's that thing there?" another said.

Someone lit a candle, and Marianne saw the room clearly:

She was smushed against one Richard Lowell, into whose nightshirt she was currently sobbing. She quickly wiped her eyes on the back of her hand and relinquished Mr. Lowell. "What happened?" she said, her voice cracked from crying.

"We heard you screaming bloody murder, that's what," George said. "We thought someone was trying to kill you!"

"Not someone, that," Arthur said. He was kneeling on Marianne's bed and poking at what Marianne now recognized as the dripping head of a large doe, cut crudely around the neck and suspended rather ingeniously above the bed. Blood had pooled beneath the severed head and was currently staining the sheets. Marianne looked down and realized she was, likewise, covered in blood.

"But I locked the door," Marianne said. "No one could have gotten in." She was embarrassed to find herself still shaking, tears leaking from her eyes.

"We know," Arthur said. "We about had to bust it down to get through." He gestured toward the door, which was hanging limply from its hinges. The three men had battered it open.

The sight of the door startled Marianne perhaps more than that of the deer's head, perhaps because the deer was obviously horrible. But the door, something so familiar, now awry on its hinges, had only the suggestion of wrongness, and that, somehow made her more afraid. She began to shake in earnest.

Pull it together, she told herself. But she couldn't. It wasn't normal to wake to find oneself eye to eye with a decapitated deer. It wasn't normal to be dragged from one's bedroom as it was engulfed in flames. It wasn't normal to be left ten thousand pounds by one's distant relation. None of this was normal, and she couldn't control any of it and—and—

She buried her head back in Richard Lowell's shirtfront and sobbed.

Then she felt someone rather awkwardly patting her back. She gritted her teeth and summoned what shreds of courage remained. "Forgive me," she said.

"It's all right," Richard said.

"Yes, you've had a shock," Arthur said. "I would be crying too, if it were me."

"As would I," George said.

Marianne nodded, smiling a little at their attempts to make her feel less like a victim.

"Someone's sending you a message," Richard said grimly. "They want you out of here."

"But who?" Marianne said.

"Maybe the deer will give us a clue," George said. "The coagulation of the blood could tell us what time it was killed."

"Yes," Richard said, releasing Marianne. She realized he had been holding her arms steady. "Let me look at the cut. That might tell us what kind of implement was used to butcher this creature."

As they gathered around the deer, which was continuously dripping onto the bed, Marianne remained where she stood, arms held tight to her chest. The room was lightening gradually as the sun rose, but still everything had a bluish chill, a predawn unfamiliarity, and that, coupled with the unnerving sensation of being covered in another creature's blood, made Marianne shiver in place.

Then, almost so quickly that Marianne didn't register it, the door to the closet opened, and from it emerged a person shrouded in a dark hood, who promptly pushed past Marianne and made for the staircase.

Marianne was all out of screams and so gestured mutely at the person who had just escaped.

Richard was the first to leap from the bed and run toward the figure. "After him!" he cried, abandoning the candle on the side table. The three men rushed toward the door and out into the staircase. Marianne could hear their footsteps as they lunged down the stairs.

Running past the limply hanging door, Marianne followed them down the hall and the stairs. She was just on the landing when she heard the sounds of a scuffle.

"Get him!" Richard shouted. "Don't let him escape, George!"

Marianne ran into the Great Hall in time to see Arthur and George wrangling the cloaked figure to the ground. Richard, who appeared to have been bashed quite hard in the face by a thrown samovar, approached the figure and threw off the hood.

"Mrs. Grubert!" Marianne said.

It was, indeed, the housekeeper. Her hair was disheveled, her face was blotchy with tears, and she looked every bit her age. "I'm sorry, Miss Keyes," Mrs. Grubert said, and through her shock, Marianne felt both pity and anger.

"Why were you lurking around in Miss Keyes' closet?" Richard demanded.

Mrs. Grubert was crying. "I'm sorry," she said. "I'm sorry. Young miss, you must forgive me."

"We'll see about that," Arthur said. "Answer the man's question."

"It was me who hung the deer's head," Mrs. Grubert said through a cascade of tears. "And it was me who lit the fire."
Marianne had known it was possible. After all, Mrs. Grubert had the keys to the house, and Marianne had no claim on the woman's loyalty, besides being a distant relation. But still, to learn that the woman had knowingly terrorized her was too much.

Marianne had to sit down.

"How could you do it?" she said at last. "Why would you do it?"

"To scare you away, why else?" Mrs. Grubert said. George was still holding her arm, but Arthur had relinquished her, and so she had to be helped to her feet. "I only lit the fire to scare you," she said. "I never meant for it to endanger you, honestly. But it got out of hand. And when nearly being burned alive didn't frighten you away, I got scared and took a butcher knife to one of Hamish's deer. I thought that if anything would scare you, it was waking up to that."

"How did you manage to string it up like that over the bed?" Arthur said.

"Yes, did you use a pulley system?" George said.

"No, sir," Mrs. Grubert said. "Only I am stronger than I look, and I dosed the young miss with laudanum in the tea I gave her."

Marianne recalled the vivid dream, the haze of awakening. Laudanum—well, now she could truly say opiates were not for her.

"But why did you want to frighten me away?" Marianne said. "Have I harmed you in some way or done you some wrong?"

"No, ma'am, nothing like that," Mrs. Grubert said. "Only I, if you knew what happened the last time a young miss lived in this house, you wouldn't be asking me how I could do all this. You'd be asking how quick you could get away!"

"But why did you linger in the closet?" Arthur said, brows knit with consternation. "Why not flee while Marianne slept?"

"Aye, I tried," Mrs. Grubert said. "The door was locked. I couldn't go out the window—it was too far to drop."

"But the door only locks from the inside," Marianne said. "How could you have been locked in?"

"That's what I'm telling you," Mrs. Grubert said. "There are strange things happening in this house, young miss. Strange and wrong things: doors locking that shouldn't. Letters sent but never arriving. I've put one thing one place, turned around, only to find it gone, with no trace."

"Well, Mrs. Grubert," Richard said, settling into a chair. "I would suggest you either tell us the whole history of this house or you will find yourself unemployed and unhoused very quickly."

Mrs. Grubert sighed. "Very well, sir. But don't say I didn't warn you about this place."

Chapter Eight: Mrs. Grubert's Tale

As angry as Marianne was at Mrs. Grubert, she couldn't help but feel a little sorry for her. The woman was clearly distraught as she kneaded her hands, recounting her tale. But then Marianne remembered that she was drenched in deer blood, and her sympathy evaporated.

"When your great-uncle got married, it was a shock to everyone," Mrs. Grubert said. "He was never right after his time abroad. I mean, not right in the head. But then he came back from the East with his new bride and…we all thought he was ready to settle down. And his new wife was beautiful, the prettiest woman that had been seen around. They were happy, for a while. But then he got called away to business—"

"Called away where?" Richard said.

"The Caribbean, sir," Mrs. Grubert said. "Mind, I was just a child when all this happened, but I remember it well. He owned property in some place, I think Antigua."

Richard visibly changed, or at least Marianne thought he did. Something strange came across his face, an expression of both surprise and discomfort. "Go on," he said to Mrs. Grubert. "I assume he had plantations there."

Marianne couldn't help but jolt in her seat. Plantations? No one had ever mentioned her uncle as having owned plantations.

"I don't know, sir," Mrs. Grubert said. "But when he went away, the mistress was very low. When she learned she was with child, she wrote to him, and he promised to return as soon as he could, but strange things started happening around here. It was like, well, some people said…"

"Said what?" George asked. He had relaxed his hold on Mrs. Grubert but still stood behind her, as if expecting her to try to run again. Arthur was seated at the table, chin in his hands, his handsome face alert. His interest was clearly piqued.

"Some said this house was cursed," Mrs. Grubert said.

"Cursed how?" Richard asked.

"They said…" Mrs. Grubert hesitated.

"Out with it," Richard said sharply.

"That any woman who entered was in mortal danger," Mrs. Grubert whispered. "And if she had the misfortune to be with child, her life was surely forfeit."

The sentence hung in the air.

"They said this because Mrs. Lavinia died?" Marianne asked.

Mrs. Grubert nodded, tears covering her cheeks. "I was there, though I was a little girl." "You said you weren't there," Marianne said.

"I lied," Mrs. Grubert said, shoulders shaking a little. "My mother couldn't have kept me away. The whole household loved Mrs. Lavinia. It was awful when she died."

"And her child?" Marianne asked.

"Lived a few days, then died," Mrs. Grubert said. "Your uncle never got to hold him."

"But what makes you think all that was caused by a curse?" Arthur asked. It was growing light, and the sun shining through the window illuminated his cherubic head of curls. He looked very young, and it seemed strange to Marianne that he was discussing death and curses. But mostly she kept wishing Richard Lowell were beside her. She very much wished she could cling to him. Then she banished the thought. She was thinking crazy. What was she, a fifteen-year-old girl? No, she was a woman with, hopefully, some sense. She didn't need to start sobbing like a child again. She needed to be logical.

"The curse talk started some time ago," Mrs. Grubert said, looking at Marianne. "Your great-uncle said it was all the fault of Henry the Eighth."

"How so?" George said, taking a renewed interest. He was a lover of history. (All men named George are.)

Mrs. Grubert paused, as if hesitating in her story.

"Say what you know," Richard said.

"It was rumored…rumored, mind you, that when Henry VIII turned the Catholics out of the country, he gave this land to a lord in his favor, your ancestor."

"My ancestor?" Marianne said.

"Aye, ma'am," Mrs. Grubert said.

"I suppose the monks weren't happy about that," Arthur said.

"No, sir," Mrs. Grubert said. "There's talk to this day that they put a curse on this place, that it resists all efforts to be made into a home. That it remains hospitable to men only, and only pure women."

"Pure?" Arthur said.

"She means celibate," Marianne said, feeling awkward to say the word but also having no desire to prolong awkwardness by dancing around it. "Virgins."

"Could any of this have been the result of chance?" George said. "Women die in childbirth often enough."

"Cheers, George," Arthur muttered.

"Well, they do," George said. "I never said it wasn't tragic."

"Aye, perhaps," Mrs. Grubert said. "But Miss," she said, looking again at Marianne with sharp eyes. "The curse, if it's real, was never lifted. I'm sure it's still in effect. If you remain at Rothmore, who's to say you won't also fall victim?"

"Surely, you don't think the curse is real?" Richard said. "That's beyond ridiculous."

"It's said the curse will linger until the property is returned to the Church," Mrs. Grubert said, still staring at Marianne. "That any women will be prey. That means you, now."

Marianne struggled to decipher her own feelings. She didn't believe in curses. Did she? The Bible spoke of curses. But it also spoke of all witchcraft being of the devil. Surely, she couldn't believe in superstitious nonsense, especially Catholic, superstitious nonsense.

"Mrs. Grubert, you well know," Marianne said at last, "that a condition of my inheritance was my remaining at Rothmore. If I leave, I will forfeit money that my great-uncle left to me."

"Cursed money, ma'am," Mrs. Grubert said. "Please, leave while you can."

"Aren't you a distant relation of the old man?" Richard said, examining Mrs. Grubert as if she were a puzzle he was unraveling. He remembered Marianne telling him as much. "Couldn't you stand to inherit if Marianne forfeits the inheritance?"

Mrs. Grubert was silent.

"Answer him," George said.

"Aye, sir," Mrs. Grubert said. "A little. But believe me, that's not my motive. I just can't stand to see another young woman killed off in this house!"

Richard beckoned for Arthur and George to join him a few paces away. "Do we believe the woman?" he asked in low tones.

"Of course not," George said. "The curse is obviously nonsense, the invention of a rural and undiscerning mind."

But Arthur hesitated. "This has all gone a bit sideways, Richard. I don't like any of this. I mean, curses? Dead children? Fires in the night? It's a bit much. I say we get out of here while we can, drop Marianne off wherever she came from originally. And try to forget this whole thing."

"And forfeit the money?" Richard hissed.

"The money isn't worth dying from a monk's curse!" Arthur said. "You, of all people, should know to steer clear of blood money."

"That's below the belt, Arthur," Richard said with a sort of repressed anger. "My father's business no longer has anything to do with me."

"Don't start on that again," George muttered as Richard and Arthur glared at each other.

Marianne, who could hear only their angry whispers, felt very left out of the discussion. None of them seemed interested in what she wanted. But it was her decision, wasn't it? If she wanted to stick it out at Rothmore, then she had a right to. Maybe it was this, more than anything, that reignited what remained of her courage: seeing them in a huddle, deciding things, while she was left outside the circle.

"Gentlemen," she said. They did not hear her. "Gentlemen," she repeated, this time more clearly.

Richard stopped mid-whisper. "Yes, Miss Keyes?"

"I will be remaining at Rothmore for the present," Marianne said.

"But—" Arthur and Mrs. Grubert said simultaneously. Richard said nothing, only stared at Marianne with a furrowed brow.

"I will be remaining," Marianne said. "The danger, however, may very well be real. So I invite, in fact, encourage, you three to leave. I cannot knowingly endanger anyone else. But I will take my chances here."

"But what about the curse?" Arthur said.

Marianne shook her head. "I will find a way to break it. If it exists," she said. "Mrs. Grubert," she said to the housekeeper, who had not moved, "you are summarily dismissed."

Mrs. Grubert nodded, as if she had been expecting this.

And Marianne went outside. She needed to clean herself and, with Mrs. Grubert leaving, the water wasn't going to appear in her bath by itself.

As she passed Hamish at the well, she saw him stare at her bloody appearance. "I am all right, Hamish," Marianne said. "But there is a large, severed doe's head in my room. If you could make haste to remove it, I would be most grateful."

Hamish blinked, and then nodded. "Yes, ma'am."

And Marianne began the process of gathering water that she wasn't sure would entirely make her clean.

Chapter Nine: An Unexpected Visitor

After Marianne left the room and Mrs. Grubert also departed in a swirl of her dark cloak, Richard, George, and Arthur were left alone.

"Ms. Keyes is either the dumbest woman or the most stubborn in the whole world," Richard said.

"Or the bravest," George said.

Richard nodded.

"Well?" Arthur said. "Let's get out of here."

Richard grabbed his friend's arm. "Wait a minute."

"Wait for what?" Arthur said.

"The danger has passed, now that the crazed housekeeper isn't running around," Richard said. "And if it hasn't—"

There was a long pause.

"We have to stay," Richard said at last. "Otherwise we're right back where we started, with no money, no prospects, no heiress."

"Richard, there are other heiresses," Arthur said.

"Yes, but we've already become invested here," Richard said. "We might as well see this thing through, for better or worse."

George and Arthur exchanged a curious glance.

"What?" Richard said.

"Richard," George said cautiously. "Is it possible—"

"Possible that you are beginning to worry for the safety of Marianne?" Arthur said.

"What? No!" Richard said. He fumbled with his words. "This is the practical, logical decision: we stay. Let's not waste our invested time, that's all I'm saying."

Arthur and George looked at each other in a way that Richard found very annoying. "What?" Richard said.

Arthur shrugged. "Whatever you say, Richard."

"I'm telling the truth!" Richard said, his blood pressure rising in direct correlation with the number of glances George and Arthur were exchanging.

"So you're not, for the record, at all concerned about the safety of Marianne Keyes?" Arthur said.

"Maybe slightly," Richard said. "My heart isn't made of stone. But really, my decision is based on a logical analysis of the situation."

"Right," George said.

"It is!" Richard said.

"Whatever you say," Arthur said.

"If we're staying," George said, sensing that Richard's blood pressure was reaching boiling point, "We better make sure this curse isn't real."

"And we better get someone to cook something," Arthur said. "I'm bloody starving."

"Anyone craving venison?" George said. "We could probably cook that head."

"Don't be revolting, George," Arthur said.

"How do we do that?" Richard said.

"Cook the venison?" George said.

"No, not that," Richard said. "Make sure there's no merit to this…curse story?"

"We look for anything the old man may have written down," Richard said at last, answering his own question. "I think it's time for another trip to the attic."

The trip to the attic proved fruitful. Richard found, among other things, yet another portrait of the late Mrs. Lavinia Babbage, as well as a trunk which he could not, for the life of him, pry open. Arthur and George both took their turns, but the trunk was stubborn. They finally had to enlist Hamish's help. The groundskeeper succeeded where they had failed: taking a massive crowbar to the trunk, he, through sheer strength, battered open the hinges, until the trunk's lid popped cleanly off.

The dining room, where these maneuvers were occurring, became coated in a layer of dust as the contents of the trunk dissipated into the air.

"Fine time to have let go of the housekeeper," Arthur muttered.

"Don't worry about dust," Richard said. "Just read." Because inside the trunk, there was indeed a large volume—a diary, as it became clear.

"It's Babbage's," Richard said, flipping through the large, dusty volume.

"What's in it?" George said, peering over Richard's shoulder.

"Papers," Richard said. "Property titles."

"So he was the rightful owner of Rothmore?" George said.

"Appears so," Richard said.

Hamish, who had been lingering, spoke uninvited for the first time: "Folks around here were very curious about how the family came to have this place."

"Really?" Richard said. "Was the old man secretive about it?"

"Aye," Hamish said through his beard. "This whole countryside was full of monks a few centuries back. Of course, that all changed. But it's hard to forget the past when you live in a place like this."

"Yes, I suppose so," Richard said.

George and Arthur exchanged significant glances.

It was then that Marianne entered. She had managed to clean herself. Her hair was still wet however, and she had, given the general informality of the situation, chosen to let it dry down.

Richard, who had never seen Marianne in such a state, was taken aback. At first, he wasn't sure she was the same person. With her hair up, Marianne appeared—not stern, but rigid, with a certain aloofness that read as coldness. With her hair down, she appeared…different. Warmer.

"I was able to get most of the blood out," Marianne said, wringing her hair in the exact way her mother had always begged her not to. "But there is a lingering smell. I'm sorry if it offends you."

"You're excused," Arthur said.

Richard refocused. "Um, we found this in the attic," he said, nodding to the volume. "It's your great-uncle's title to the house. It traces the house back to roughly the time of Henry VIII."

Marianne blanched. "So my ancestors did inherit this place after the monks were expelled?"

"The timelines do add up," George said. "Your ancestors would have begun living here roughly after the monks were allowed to leave."

"That's an interesting choice of words," Arthur muttered.

"They haven't yet invented a polite word for being violently expelled from your home," George retorted.

Arthur had to concede that point.

"I don't know anything about all this," Marianne said. "Father's always had some sympathies for the Catholic Church. He sometimes attended lectures on the subject. They weren't open to women, though." Now she was wishing she had attended, even if against his wishes. Maybe she would have learned something useful. "Is there any mention of any other women," she swallowed, "dying here?"

"No, but—" George started.

"But women aren't likely to have many records written about them," Richard said. There wasn't particularly a nice way to say that.

Marianne nodded. "Maybe we'll be able to find another diary."

"Was someone likely to write in their diary 'I think I'm cursed by medieval monks'? Seems a little strange," Richard said.

"I don't know," Marianne said. "I've written some strange things in mine. Or I will have, once I get around to writing about the last few days."

"There!" George said, stabbing a finger at a page in a massive, crumbling bible, whose inner cover was full of scribbled dates. They all peered at the writing, barely discernible on the faded text: Mrs. Joshua Babbage, died abed. Child survived three days.

"When was this?" Marianne asked, fighting to repress a shudder.

"Doesn't say," Richard said.

"There!" Arthur said, pointing to a page, on which another entry was written: Mrs. Mary Merton, died Christmas morning.

"She must have been a visitor," Marianne said.

Hamish, who had remained, startled them by speaking: "Aye, I remember now, it was also said that female servants shouldn't stay in the house. They were always made to sleep in the village."

"This is the hardest working curse I've ever heard of," Arthur said, "if it's killing off not only members of the family, but any women associated at all with this house."

"Hamish, you knew about this?" Marianne said. "You knew about the curse?"

Hamish shifted. "Aye, ma'am. In my grandfather's time, it was talked about often. But that was all long ago."

Marianne began to put the pieces together in her mind. "I don't know what to make of any of this," she said. "I dislike superstition. I mean, we're in the era of enlightenment, aren't we? We shouldn't have to be afraid of shadows. There must be some scientific way to test this curse theory."

"If this is true—" Richard began.

"We don't know it's true," George said.

"No, but let's say Marianne is correct," Richard said. "Maybe we should perform an experiment."

They stood around the book, all without suggestions.

It was then that they heard the distinct sound of steps in the hallway.

Marianne glanced at Richard.

"I thought you sent the woman away?" Richard said.

"I did," Marianne said.

"Then who—" Richard began.

There was a knock on the door.

Marianne tried to calm herself. A ghost wouldn't knock. She took a deep breath and opened the door. What greeted her both shocked and surprised her—

In the doorway stood her friend, Madelyn, dressed for traveling.

"Madelyn!" Marianne said.

"Marianne!" Madelyn said.

They screamed and embraced, a girlish glee overwhelming them. Jumping while still maintaining a hug was challenging, but not impossible, as they proved.

"What are you doing here?" Marianne asked breathlessly when they'd finally stopped jumping.

"My father had to come to England to meet with a Bishop," Madelyn said breathlessly. "I got your letter in London. My aunt hadn't sent it to Majorca yet. I read all about the strange goings-on here, and I knew I had to come!"

"Are you here alone?" Arthur said, interjecting.

"Well, not now. I'm with you all," Madelyn said.

"No, but I mean that you traveled here alone?" Arthur said.

"Quite alone," Madelyn said.

"Is that safe?" George said.

"Quite safe!" Madelyn said.

"What if you'd been attacked, or set upon by highwaymen?" Richard said.

"Highwaymen!" Madelyn said, laughing delightedly. "In this little hamlet! That's the most ludicrous thing I've ever heard!"

The three gentlemen exchanged sheepish looks.

"It's not that unbelievable," Richard said, sounding a little miffed.

Madelyn winked at Marianne. "I've been halfway around the horn of Africa, and they think I shy away from a ride in a coach!"

Marianne felt the need to explain to the gawking gentlemen. "Madelyn's parents are missionaries," she said. "You won't find a more well-traveled woman than her. She doesn't adhere to the usual proprieties around women's travel."

"Oh yes," Madelyn said. "I've been to India and Africa and…oh, yes, Putney. Of the three, Putney was the least hospitable." She spotted Hamish. "Is that beard real? Can I tug it?" Without waiting for an answer, she tugged it and Hamish, who was understandably startled, blushed beneath his whiskers. "Oh, it is real!" Madelyn said.

"Is she always like this?" Richard said to Marianne.

"No, she's usually much more energetic," Marianne said, "but I expect she's tired from traveling." She was watching her friend like someone would watch an excitable puppy.

"But tell me—" Madelyn said, dragging Marianne to a chair, "what's been happening here?"

Marianne recounted the events of the past days, including Mrs. Grubert's claim of a curse and Marianne's desire to test the theory.

"Then the solution is obvious!" Madelyn said.

This had been the last thing Marianne was expecting. "Is it?" Marianne said.

"Of course!" Madelyn said. "We just find a pregnant person and have them come here."

"But how?" Marianne said.

"Well, we know how," Arthur said cheekily. "Richard definitely does."

"Um," Richard said, redness flooding his face. "I-I don't think that's going to be possible. We shouldn't risk someone else's safety by enticing them here." He made a point of not looking at Marianne.

"Just my safety," Madelyn said.

"You chose to come here!" Marianne said. "I technically didn't invite you."

"All right, all right," Madelyn said. "I suppose that's true."

"What if—" Arthur said, after a moment's thought, "What if we indulged the house?"

"Indulged how?" Richard said.

"By making it think we're men!" Madelyn said, leaping to her feet in excitement. "Marianne, we'll trick the house!"

"That's silly," Marianne said. "The house isn't sentient. It can't perceive our sex."

"Do you have a better idea?" Madelyn said.

Marianne did not.

Madelyn turned to the gentlemen in the room. "Do you have spare clothes we could wear?"

"Our trunks, sadly, have yet to arrive," Richard lied smoothly.

Hamish came to the rescue. "Aye, I've got some things you could wear. It'll be a bit ill-fitting, though."

"We can make it suit," Madelyn said. "Come on, Marianne. What do you say?"

Marianne considered. The whole idea of "tricking" a house sounded absurd. But if it helped her keep her ten thousand pounds, then she was willing to try it.

"All right," she said. "Let's man up."

Chapter Ten: The House Turns

Folded into a thick shirt and breeches rather too tight around her hips, Marianne sat in the downstairs parlor, sipping tea she had made, and not particularly well. She didn't even know how it was possible to mess up tea, but she had managed it. The others were polite enough not to mention it. Except Richard, who appeared to be very moodily consuming the least amount possible.

"Just five men here, sitting," Madelyn said loudly, looking around, as if the house were silently taking notes. Marianne's friend had donned one of Marianne's late uncle's old uniforms. It was almost unnerving how at home Madelyn looked in military garb. Marianne could picture her riding into battle very comfortably.

"This is asinine," George muttered.

"Don't be a spoilsport," Madelyn said.

"Yeah, George," Arthur said, grinning under his mustache. "Don't be a spoilsport."

"The house can't hear us," George said. "It's a house."

"Places have feelings too," Madelyn said.

"I think you've been too long gone from England," George said. "You veer into fantasy."

"Don't be so sure," Madelyn said, sounding unbothered. "It wasn't that long ago that even Englishmen, and women, believed completely in faeries and goblins and magical goings-on. They couldn't all have been wrong."

"I thought you were Christian," George said.

"I am. But it's important to have an open mind when dealing with these things," Madelyn said.

"Who made her the expert in curses?" George said to no one.

"Calm down, George," Madelyn said. "Your neck is getting red."

"It is not!" George said. (It was.)

"Marianne," Richard said, "I need to show you something. In the library."

"Another of my uncle's books?" Marianne said, but then she felt stupid. Books generally were the things found in libraries.

"Indeed," Richard said.

Arthur and George no doubt would have exchanged significant glances, but George was rather occupied with disproving Madelyn's theories. After a long, angry sip, he said, "Just because the Mohammedan religions posit a different sort of spirituality, you can't then make the leap to their endorsing the sort of anthropomorphizing you're engaging in!"

"I'm just saying that it doesn't hurt to recognize the spiritual context of a place, including a property like this one!" Madelyn said.

Richard shut the door to the parlor, and suddenly he and Marianne were in silence. Neither of them broke it as they made their way to the library, in which Hamish had built up a fire. The sight of it cheered Marianne. She wished her sisters were there, to gather around it with her and poke at the ashes with a stick. She missed the easy domesticity of the past and found herself now afflicted with a strange series of emotions: curiosity, however, was foremost.

"Where's the book you wanted to show me?" Marianne said.

Richard had, of course, been lying. There was no book. "I wanted, first, to ask—" he struggled within himself. "Are you sure you shouldn't leave?"

Marianne was silent, and he couldn't read her expression.

"I don't know if the curse is real," Richard said. "And I'm not inherently superstitious. But I believe in sensible precautions. Given what Mrs. Grubert said, and given that you are, in fact, a woman, would it not be better? That is, perhaps it would be wisest…for you to leave."

Marianne could have asked any number of questions. Why did he feel it was his place to give her advice? Did he think these breeches looked as ridiculous on her as she suspected they did? But instead she found herself asking: "Do you want me to leave?"

"I don't . . . I mean, this is your house," Richard said. "I remain here at your discretion. If you leave, I also would leave."

"Where would you go?" Marianne asked. She was surprised that she was so curious to know his answer.

"I suppose, London," Richard said.

"Not the Lake District?"

"The Lake District? Oh, right. No, no, that plan has been abandoned. Since we've been sidetracked," Richard said.

Marianne traced her fingers along the bust Mrs. Grubert had shown her earlier. The texture of the marble was smooth.

"This has been a very strange few days," Marianne said. "Very strange."

"Would you have a place to go? If you did decide to leave?" Richard asked.

"Back to Dair, I suppose," Marianne said. "To my parents'. But I can't leave. Not with my inheritance tied up in this place."

"But how could you hope to have any kind of future here?" Richard said. "You can never hope to have children, not with that grim curse business hanging over your head. Not that I believe it, but—" he trailed off, unsure what point he was making.

"I never expect to have children," Marianne said. "So I won't be in danger from that."

"Why not?" Richard asked. "Don't you want children?"

Marianne paused. "Want is a strange word," she said. "I do like children, but I just don't expect to have any."

"Why not?" Richard persisted. He knew he wasn't being very gentlemanly or charming, but his curiosity got the better of him. He wanted to know.

"Because—" Marianne struggled to know how to say something rather personal to Richard Lowell without it feeling like an admission of something. "Generally, one gets married before having children. And I never plan to marry."

"Why not?" Richard asked.

Marianne tried and failed to think of some way to extricate herself cleanly from this conversation. She had no desire to admit her emotional misgivings to Richard Lowell, insulter of blue dresses and clergyman's daughters. But she also felt stuck, or rather, unable to leave.

Marianne sat down on a divan, and Richard, not wanting to loom over her, sat beside her, then regretted it when their knees almost touched, and the sensation pained him. Well, not pained him. But it was a strong sensation, almost like—

"Generally, women marry who have money, or beauty, or great talent," Marianne said. "I do not have the fortune of being blessed with those traits."

"You have money," Richard said.

Marianne was startled to realize that she did, in fact, now have money. "I suppose so," she said.

The next part slipped out before he could weigh the merits of venturing it: "And you have beauty."

Marianne had never heard anyone say that about her, and so was entirely unprepared. Her instincts betrayed her, and she said, before she could stop herself, "That's not true."

"What?" Richard said.

"I don't…I mean, you're too kind," Marianne said, trying in vain to regain some control over the situation.

"You are beautiful," Richard said. Then, honesty getting the better of him, he added, "Though not in a conventional sense."

"Then how?" Marianne said. She was frightened to ask this, and had to hide her hands, which may have been shaking, beneath a pillow, forcing them into fists. She missed her skirts. She could have hidden her clenched fists in their folds.

"Like a very old portrait of someone I should know but don't," Richard said. "Your face has a foreignness. I don't mean un-English, exactly, but… I would never guess that you were from a little countryside village. You resemble too much some figment of imagination, some strange creature of fantasy. An imp, perhaps."

"Like, a nice imp?" Marianne said.

"I can't tell," Richard said. "I've never seen anyone ever with your face. It is completely unique."

Marianne nodded, unsure if this was a compliment. "You look completely average," she sighed. "The epitome of an English nobleman's bored son."

"I am an English nobleman's bored son," Richard said. Their knees were touching, and Richard had to stare ahead, to avoid fixating on her eyes, which were uncomfortably large and now, inexplicably, filling with tears.

"What's wrong?" he said, alarmed.

"I don't know," Marianne said, honestly. Maybe it was the prolonged strain of the past few days, the strangeness of her circumstances, or maybe it was the proximity of, the irony of, a man who had called her both ugly and beautiful. How was she to trust either statement? Why should she care? If the curse does exist, she thought, now would be a very convenient time for it to kill her. She would welcome the escape from this conversation.

Richard's instinct when confronted with crying women was, as it always had been, to kiss them. And yes, this rarely ended well. He seized Marianne's hand and kissed the palm, which was wet because she had wiped her eyes with it.

"Marianne," he said, "if the prospect wouldn't endanger you, I would—" But his polished phrases died in his throat. He couldn't summon his well-worn flirtations, and this panicked him. He let go of her hand because his had begun to sweat.

"We should rejoin the others," Marianne said, standing abruptly.

Richard stood. "Marianne," he managed at last, "about that inheritance—" This too died in his throat. He needed to make his move, to ingratiate himself to her once and for all, but practicality eluded him. Instead, as if he were once again sixteen, figuring out women for the first time, he found himself launching himself at her face clumsily, awkwardly, like a pubescent teenager motivated by hormones, not experience.

Richard kissed, not her mouth, but the side of her mouth, in a rather strange gesture. The contact lasted all of two seconds and when he recovered himself, he was startled by the sight of red. "Marianne, you're bleeding!" he said.

Her fingers went instinctively to the site of his sticky, sideways kiss. "Your mustache," she said.

It seemed a wiry, errant strand of his mustache had actually, freakishly, broken the delicate skin of her lower cheek. "Oh," he said. "Marianne, I'm sorry—"

"No, it's all right," she said. "I'm sorry."

"For what?" he said.

"I got tear-stains on your collar," she said.

"Don't worry about that," he said instinctively, retrieving from his pocket a handkerchief, which he applied to her lower cheek.

All of which was strange in and of itself, but was made even stranger, when, at the moment Richard touched Marianne for the third time, the very large portrait of Great Uncle Babbage, previously hung above the fireplace, fell from the wall and crashed to the ground, the frame erupting in slivers.

Marianne screamed and then, embarrassed of having screamed, covered her mouth with her hands. Richard reached for a pistol he didn't have and ended up pointing his finger, rather ineffectually, at the fragments of the portrait frame. "What the—" he breathed.

And Richard knew, though he could not have proven it, but knew rather in the way that an animal knew when it was in danger, that the portrait had fallen because he had touched Marianne.

When George, Arthur, and Madelyn appeared in the doorway, summoned by the loud noise of the crash, they found Marianne and Richard, very circumspectly on opposite sides of the room, beginning to pick up the fragments of the frame and pretending as if the house weren't determined to kill her.

Madelyn and Marianne shed their breeches in the bedroom and donned their old dresses.

"It was worth a try," Marianne said.

"I really thought the house would go for that," Madelyn said with a sigh. "But it seems not."

"Is there any other way to break a curse?" Marianne said.

"Do you have a clergyman handy?" Madelyn said.

"I could ask my father to come," Marianne said. "But he's, you know, a rector, and it would take him ages to arrive."

"What about in the village?" Madelyn said.

"Probably," Marianne said. "I haven't asked yet."

"No time like the present," Madelyn said. "Maybe he could do something."

"Like what?" Marianne asked.

"I don't know," Madelyn said. "Doesn't hurt to ask, though."

Having no better plan herself, Marianne found herself agreeing. Besides, a trip to Bickersmore was much needed. She was very hungry, and food wasn't going to make itself.

When Marianne and Madelyn announced their plans to find the clergy of Bickersmore and beg them to come to the house and "fix it", whatever that might entail, the three gentlemen insisted on going along, in part out of a performative chivalry, in part out of boredom, and in part because (though they vehemently denied this) the house was starting to scare them a little.

"The house won't hurt you, you know," Madelyn said shrewdly, looking at the three men as they hurried outside onto the gravel path that led away from the house. "You're not women. What do you have to worry about?"

They pretended not to hear her and instead began remarking about the weather. These remarks soon proved prescient.

The walk to Bickersmore passed rather slowly, because the recent rains had left certain sections of road flooded. It became necessary for the gentlemen to carry the women across some sections, which was of course very awkward, because it involved touching.

Richard was encouraged by George and Arthur to carry Marianne across what amounted to an oversized puddle, which, despite her protestations, he agreed to do.

"This is humiliating," she said, as she bridal-carried her several yards. "I don't mind a bit of mud."

"Stop wriggling," he said, rather out of breath.

"Don't tell me I'm heavy," Marianne said with a sigh. "No woman wants to hear that."

"I wasn't going to," he said. "It's just that, strangely enough, my diet of alcohol and dissipation had left my arms a little worse for wear, and it's possible I'm not quite as"—he paused to navigate a swell in the road—"strong as I once was."

"A symptom of your effete pastimes and chronic ennui?" Marianne asked, perhaps a little rudely.

"Something like that," Richard said. "Don't tell me the clergyman's daughter disapproves of dissipation?"

"Sorry to be so predictable, but yes, I do," Marianne said. She found herself trying to suck in her stomach, completely illogically, as if that would make her less heavy. Why she cared if Richard thought she was heavy, she didn't know.

"Dissipation is wonderfully fun if you've got the money for it," Richard said. "Bloody expensive habit though, if you've not."

"Have you gotten into worse scrapes than this?" Marianne said. "Worse than murderous houses?" She was curious in spite of herself.

"Yes," he said, only half-lying. "I'm a veteran of such scrapes. This is just another week of adventure for me."

"Your life must be very active and exciting," Marianne said.

Richard was about to answer in the affirmative, but the truth writhed its way into him, and he found himself being unpleasantly honest: "Not really. At some point, when you're excavating roaches from your bed for the third time in a week in the filthiest inn in Putney, you wish you lived a life just a tad more stable."

The total absence of charm in his reply alarmed him. How were his powers of flirtation deserting him so entirely? What had come over him? He strove to recover quickly, as they were nearly at the point where he could have to put Marianne down. "I mean, rather," he said, "that I long for the stability of home and hearth. You know, domesticity. To see the shining faces of offspring surrounding me."

"Do you think that's realistic?" Marianne asked. "That someone who lived such a peripatetic existence should then become a solid, upstanding citizen with the burdens of children and wife? It seems like quite a shift for anyone."

Richard was just struggling for a response when Marianne wriggled free of his grip, and he had to set her down. (The muscles of his arms were very relieved.)

They reached the end of the flooded section of road just as a downpour commenced and Marianne, Richard, Arthur (who had been ferrying a protesting Madelyn), Madelyn, and George, were forced to run for it, finally arriving at the village of Bickersmore soaked and winded.

They took refuge in a haberdashery, where they learned that the most proximate clergyman, a vicar named Mr. Blithes, resided in a cottage, where he was currently at supper.

Madelyn suggested they try their luck with a direct appeal, and she and Marianne wrung out their hats and hair as best they could, before arriving at the clergyman's doorstep. They were told to enter by a kindly-looking housekeeper and bidden to sit in a parlor.

"Don't sit!" Madelyn hissed, just as Arthur was descending toward a settee. "Your backside is soaked through!"

"Madam," Arthur said with a strained formality, "worry about your own backside." And he sat anyway.

The vicar appeared in the doorway at that very moment "backsides" were mentioned.

Arthur sprang to his feet. "Mr. Blithes!" he said. The others turned to face the clergyman, a very mild-looking, elderly gentleman.

"Hello," he said.

"Mr. Blithes," Marianne said, feeling the need to steer them away from backsides, "I am Marianne Keyes. I recently inherited Rothmore Hall. My great-uncle was Colonel Babbage."

"Oh, yes," Mr. Blithes said, and a shadow fell across his otherwise perfectly pleasant face.

Marianne, uncertain how to proceed, looked at Madelyn for help, but her friend was busy glaring at Arthur, who had again sunk into a chair and whose muddy shoes were even at that moment staining the otherwise immaculate carpet.

Richard came to her assistance. "Mr. Blithes," he said, "I am a friend of these young ladies, and have been lately staying in Rothmore Hall. We have, unfortunately, been troubled by some incidents, the nature of which we had hoped you could…" He struggled for the best word. " . . . explain."

Mr. Blithes sighed heavily and sat down in a chintz armchair. The others, following his lead, also sat.

"I would pretend not to know to what you are referring," Mr. Blithes said, "but I am too old to waste my time, and yours. The truth is, I warned your great-uncle about that house many times," he said, directing his remarks to Marianne. "But he ignored my advice on all occasions."

"Warned?" Marianne said, fear clenching her heart despite her attempts to steady herself. "Warned of what?"

"Of certain…unsavory presences," Mr. Blithes said.

"You mean spirits? Ghosts?" Arthur said.

"I won't label it, but in essence, yes," Mr. Blithes said. "I am not a superstitious man—"

"Nor am I," Richard interjected.

"Nor I," George said hastily.

"But a life in a religious vocation does teach one to accept spiritual realities beyond the visible and commonplace," Mr. Blithes said. "The miraculous and…the diabolic."

"What do you mean?" Madelyn asked.

"I mean," Mr. Blithes said, "that every young woman in that house has suffered an unpleasant fate. I warned your great-uncle not to take a wife, but he did not listen. I warned him to vacate after the death of his wife and child. Though at that point, I was concerned mostly for his health. To live a life of regrets, shut up in an estate and ruminating daily on one's past errors, is unwise." Mr. Blithes shook his head. "No, my dear, I would advise you and your friends to vacate the house immediately. Let no delay impede you."

"But—" Marianne explained the conditions of her inheritance.

Mr. Blithes had resumed shaking his head before she was through. "My dear, let no inheritance persuade you to remain in a position where your physical safety is at risk. And I assure you, in that place, it is. You would do best to leave immediately."

"Isn't there anything you could do?" Marianne said. "To…satisfy the house?"

"My dear, if it were a matter of a few simple prayers, I would oblige you instantly," Mr. Blithes said. "But I'm afraid what lurks in that house is something truly—"

They never learned what Mr. Blithes thought lurked in the house, because at that moment, the housekeeper appeared in the doorway. "Sir," she said to Mr. Blithes, "you are expected at the Robinsons, in a half hour."

"Right," Mr. Blithes said, and, struggling to rise from his chair, had to allow himself to be assisted by Richard. "Let me issue a final warning. Quite apart from anything sinister in the house, it seems unwise for five young people to be alone in a great big house on a night like this. You would do better to remain in the village."

And he shuffled off to prepare for whatever was happening at the Robinsons.

Marianne and the others had no choice but to leave.

"They didn't even offer us tea," Arthur said, audibly miffed.

"Tea? How can you think about tea?" Madelyn said. "The house is possessed!" They began picking their way back through the front garden to the main road.

"Don't you lose your nerve!" Marianne said. She needed Madelyn's courage, or she was afraid she might lose her own.

"I'm not losing my nerve," Madelyn said. "I'm just saying, we need to change tacks, that's all."

"How?" Marianne asked. It had stopped raining, and it wasn't particularly close, so she wasn't sure why exactly Richard was standing so close. She was painfully aware that his arm was touching hers. Then she felt ashamed for noticing this detail and determined not to notice it, which of course meant that she could not get it out of her mind.

"You know, in some regions of Africa," Madelyn said, "if someone or something is thought to be possessed, a witch doctor comes and performs certain rites to alleviate the suffering of the victim."

"Does it work?" Marianne said.

"Sometimes, yes," Madelyn said.

"Hogwash," George sniffed. "This is England, not Africa. And you'll find no witch doctors here."

"We could learn a thing or two from Africa in this country," Madelyn said.

"But Madelyn, we're Christians, and that all sounds rather pagan," Marianne said.

"Spiritual reality evades easy classification," Madelyn said. "Who's to say we can't accomplish something similar with Christian means?"

"Meaning what?" Richard said. They had moved out of the vicar's front garden and were now walking to the edge of the village.

"Meaning we dress it up like a monastery again," Madelyn said. "Return to the past."

"You realize the last time you played dress up, it was totally ineffectual?" Arthur said.

"I admit, I was misguided," Madelyn said. "But that's because the house doesn't want me and Marianne to be men. It wants the house to be a priory again. And we can…well, we can't actually make it a priory again, but we can pretend."

"You speak as if the house were sentient," Richard said, becoming uncomfortable.

"The house isn't," Madelyn said, "but…certain memories linger. That's all we'd be doing. Acknowledging those memories."

"Whatever you call it, it's weird," George said empathically.

"Oh come on, George," Arthur said unexpectedly. "Where's your sense of adventure? If Madelyn wants to dress us all up as monks, who are we to refuse?"

"All right," Marianne said to her friend. "Nothing else has worked. We might as well try this." She looked at Richard, George, and Arthur. "You are, as always, free to leave. I cannot guarantee your safety and I imagine, if you're feeling at all like I am, Mr. Blithes' remarks did nothing to reassure you about the success of my project."

Richard swallowed his nerves. "Don't be ridiculous. We're staying." She evaded his gaze but he thought she almost, sort of, kind of smiled.

"Fantastic!" Madelyn said. "Now, what all will we need for an impromptu midnight mass, do you think?"

Chapter Eleven: Midnight Mass

The return walk to Rothmore passed more quickly than any of them liked, even with the burdens of their purchases. It was late by the hour of their return, and they had to commence work immediately to prepare for midnight. Why midnight, they could not have said. It just felt like the right time for such a thing as they were planning.

Marianne tore down the curtains in her bedroom and commenced stitching makeshift monks' robes, which involved a lot of pricked fingers because, in the candlelight, she could not clearly see her own hands.

Richard and Arthur set about gathering all the seats in the house and making a loose equivalent to a very eclectic chapel in the great hall, where Hamish had built up a fire and, perhaps perceiving that they were up to something odd, excused himself from the house. The chairs were arranged so that, if one squinted, they resembled pews. At the front, Madelyn set about decorating a table as if it were an altar. They had no proper communion wafers and so Madelyn had to do her best approximation with the ingredients they had brought from Bickersmore, as well as what Mrs. Grubert had left behind. For sacramental wine, she substituted a bottle of something strong Mrs. Grubert had hidden in a back cabinet.

George, who disapproved of the whole enterprise, reluctantly made himself useful by studying a book on Catholic liturgy he'd found in the library. The preparations took rather longer than any of them had planned. By the time Marianne descended with the robes, Madelyn appeared with the fake eucharist, and George arrived in the main hall, it was a quarter until midnight and, except for the fireplace, quite dark.

Richard, George, and Arthur had attended a session once with the famed Dr. Mesmer, and Richard had expected this to feel similar, but it did not. While Dr. Mesmer had impressed him with his showmanship and skill, this attempt at mimicking Catholic worship felt clumsy, amateurish, and—a startling thing for an atheist like him to admit—rather blasphemous. The whole thing was unsettling.

"Marianne, are you sure about this?" he said as she handed him a curtain-turned-habit.

"No," she said.

"This all feels rather sacrilegious, doesn't it?" Richard said.

"Yes, it does," she said. "I think I won't tell my parents about this part."

Marianne, who was sincerely Christian, didn't like the idea of copying a Catholic mass. It seemed like aping or mockery in some way, but she had never felt more serious in her life. And what other way did she have to make peace with the monks who seemed to resent her presence? Would their fake mass anger them? Or would it appease them? She did not know. But either way, perhaps it would elicit a definite reaction.

There was no time to express all of this, and so Marianne said, "I think that it's best, all things considered." And they left it at that.

They all donned their robes, which weren't exactly authentic, but in the shadows, they sort of resembled proper monk garb. "I guess I'll lead us in the liturgy," George said. "Unless someone else prefers."

They all shook their heads.

"Here's the wine," Madelyn said, proffering a glass. Marianne recognized it as the glass fashioned from a skull that had, until recently, sat in her great-uncle's chambers. "It was the strangest one I could find," Madelyn said.

Did Marianne tell them its origins, that it was possibly a human skull turned cup? She did not dare.

"Wait," Marianne said, as Madelyn moved to set down the glass. "I should just add—" With a motion that appeared practiced but was not, she slit her palm open with grape scissors. The others inhaled sharply as she squeezed her hand into a fist, and great droplets of blood fell into the wine below. "They want my blood," Marianne said. "Maybe this will appease them." There was no time to bandage her hand, and so she clenched it tight and tried to ignore the throbbing of the wound. She could not have explained fully the logic that led her to do this. It simply felt appropriate as strange things, in darkened rooms, under odd circumstances, so often do.

"This is all turning rather strange," Arthur muttered to Richard as they sat down.

"That's just now occurring to you?" Richard said.

The clock struck midnight, and they all fell silent.

"A hymn to begin with," George said.

Madelyn and Marianne commenced singing "Panis Angelicus". Marianne had a decent voice, but Madelyn's was truly angelic, and so the hymn left them all feeling perhaps more than they had intended. Richard, Arthur, and George, who had not been in a church service of any description, let alone a Catholic one, in some time, were silent.

"Let's proceed," George said, and he began to read out of the book a homily and the Creed, none of which the others really understood, but the words seemed to have a solidity to them, a heaviness that could have been solemn or unsettling. At last, they arrived at the Eucharist. George began to bless the Eucharist, clumsily, in Latin, very aware that as he was not a proper priest, this was disrespectful at best, sacrilege at worst.

"I think you're supposed to come forward," he said.

They stood and made their way to the front, where George dispensed in their mouths a wafer Madelyn had made out of old bread. The taste was awful, and they swallowed quickly, eagerly following with the tainted wine simply to forget the taste of the bread.

They had done as much and Richard, remembering the stifling religious services of his youth at the taste of that awful bread, said to the air, "Well, we've done it. What more do you want from us?"

It was then that it happened. It could have been an accident. Perhaps it was. But the clock fell over, tipping not sideways, but forward, landing heavily and loudly, reverberating through the hall. Madelyn, who had the skull cup, was startled and dropped it, and it shattered completely upon contact with the floor, wine spreading outward in a hideous stain.

Marianne didn't have enough air in her lungs to scream, but she felt true terror at the sight and leapt up on a chair, trying to escape the spreading stain. The chair, without provocation, tipped over, and she landed also on the ground. This did elicit a small scream and when she rose, she was shaking so badly, she could barely run. But run she did, because Arthur shouted, as other chairs began to tumble over. "Get out of here!"

They took off in different directions. Madelyn darted down the hall, Marianne up the stairs, and Richard followed her, not consciously, but as if by instinct.

Marianne rushed into her bedroom and collapsed on her bed, only to scream at the sudden appearance of a looming silhouette in the doorway. "Marianne, it's me!" Richard said.

"Oh," she said, sitting up. She was shaking very badly and could not pretend to have any degree of emotional control. "Richard, I'm going to die," she said. "They'll kill me."

"They won't," he said. "They won't."

He was drawn to her inexplicably, and in the dark, could barely make out the shape of her face, but could still see, or thought he could see, her very large eyes. He could feel her grasping for his arm, as if searching for stability. But he couldn't offer her much. He wasn't feeling very stable himself. The whole exercise, the reference to religiosity he loathed, the drinking of her blood, the strange occurrences below, had animated him.

"Marianne," he said. "Let me kiss you."

"They'll kill me," she said, again.

"Let me kiss you," he said, and he kissed her palm, forgetting the blood on it, which tasted to him strangely piquant.

"They'll kill you," Marianne said, her mind unable to see a way out of the situation. She saw death everywhere she turned.

"That's all right," Richard answered, nonsensically, and he kissed what turned out to be her neck.

It was then that the bed collapsed. The wooden headboard gave out, as did the supports, and the mattress fell three feet to the ground, landing with a bang. Richard had fallen across Marianne and, after picking himself up, realized what had happened. "Lord, they're persistent," he muttered.

Marianne extricated herself from the bed hangings and Richard and said, "I have to leave. I have to leave now."

"Marianne!" Richard said, but she had already run out the door, and he could hear her progress down the hall.

Marianne tore down the hall, and then the stairs, where she collided with—

"Madelyn!" she said, almost crying with relief.

"A ghost thing just tried to kill me!" Madelyn said.

"Me too!" Marianne said.

"Why is your neck bloody?" Madelyn said.

"I don't—" Marianne felt where Richard had touched her neck, which still seemed to burn.

"Arthur and George are—" Madelyn began.

But Marianne no longer cared. She seized her friend's arm and ran, half-dragging her, to the front door, which she thrust open, and where she collapsed onto the gravel drive.

"Marianne?" Madelyn said, but Marianne was not conscious. Overcome by the excitement of the past days, she had, apparently, swooned.

And when she swooned, she perceived something truly strange and extraordinary.

Chapter Twelve: A Strange Agreement

Marianne was looking at Rothmore, but it was not Rothmore. Part of the west hall didn't appear to exist, and there were many people moving around outside and inside, people dressed like—

Monks.

Was this what the house had once looked like?

She could see monks plowing what she had always thought was simply a meadow. Cattle grazed in a nearby pasture.

Marianne, though ostensibly in the presence of the beings trying to kill her, could not muster up fear. She felt as if she were seeing Rothmore for the first time.

"Hello?" she said, and an abbott was in front of her, and she was in the priory as it had once been. His eyes were as before—full and black.

"Why are you in our home?" the abbott asked.

"Your home?" Marianne said. "It's not yours anymore."

"Time changes nothing," he said. "It remains ours."

"No," Marianne said, beginning to cry. "It is mine! My uncle—"

"Leave this place," he said. "Promise me this."

"And do what with it?" Marianne said.

"You cannot remain."

"Why?" Marianne demanded. Even though she knew this wasn't real, or not actually, physically happening, her anger felt real. "What have I ever done to you?"

"Nothing," the abbott said. "But the past remains. Things remain unchanged. You must leave this place."

"You wish me to return it to your church?" Marianne said, a dull feeling of certainty setting around her sternum.

The abbott nodded.

"That won't be easy," Marianne said.

"Goodbye," the abbott said. "Marianne."

"Marianne!"

She was aware of her name being shouted. But not by the abbott, who had disappeared. No, her name was coming from elsewhere. But where?

She opened her eyes to see Madelyn leaning over her. It was still night. Madelyn exhaled. "Thank goodness! You were out cold for a minute!"

Marianne sat up and became aware that she needed a blanket. Her fingers felt frozen. "I'm selling Rothmore," she said.

Chapter Thirteen: Controversy & the Garden

The next day, after Marianne had explained her strange dream or vision to the others, her decision was met, not with enthusiasm, but silence.

"You're sure?" Richard said. "You're absolutely sure this is the solution?"

"I think so," Marianne said. "It's not a perfect atonement, but it's a gesture. I'm convinced this place will never be at peace until it's returned to its proper owners."

"You mean, the church?" George said, polishing his glasses.

"Yes," Marianne said.

"Why do they get to be the proper owners?" George said. "Who's to say they didn't seize this land from someone else?"

"That's true," Madelyn said. "But they seem adamant to hold onto this place."

"So we're just completely admitting the existence of ghosts now?" George said. "What are we, in the medieval ages?"

"You were pretty convinced ghosts were real last night," Arthur said drily. "I seem to recall you crying rather loudly in a closet for someone to get them off you!"

"I was overexcited!" George said. "And you know that was just a coat that fell on top of me."

"We were all overexcited last night," Marianne said, deliberately not looking at Richard when she said this. "But what I saw had enough of the truth in it to convince me. I'm selling this place. The church won't be able to get ahold of it, most likely. Not with how things are in England at the moment. But at least I can keep other people from moving in here."

"But Marianne," Madelyn said slowly, "you must know that means you forfeit your inheritance."

"I know," Marianne said. "But no amount of money is worth being haunted by homicidal monks. It's just not. Besides, I'm not even sure I want this place anymore. It's…well, I'm not sure it really is mine, by rights."

"That's debatable," George said. "Again, why do these monks, if they are in fact spiritually extant, get to determine inheritance law? By rights, this place, the money, is yours!"

"By whose rights?" Marianne said. "Legal rights? I'm not sure the law applies in situations like this. This seems to go beyond signed documents in neat solicitors' offices. This is a matter of…of safety and morality," she said, feeling that this was rather a lofty thing to say, but what else was there to say?

Madelyn nodded. "If that's what you want, then we should probably plan to leave soon."

Marianne nodded. "Yes." She should have exited the room at this to begin packing. But she realized she was waiting to hear what Richard thought. But Richard remained silent, sitting on a divan, appearing as if his thoughts were entirely elsewhere.

Marianne followed Madelyn from the room. Madelyn, who had moved dozens of times in her life, was the acknowledged packing expert and had already began chatting about the most efficient way of arranging their trunks.

George collapsed in a chair. "What just happened?" he said. "What in the bloody hell just happened?"

"They've figured it all out, apparently," Arthur said.

"And we're not part of the equation," George said. "No money for us." He did not sound amused.

"We always knew that was a possibility," Richard said, defeated in tone and spirit.

George and Arthur looked at him incredulously. "Hang on a minute," Arthur said. "Don't you start acting like this whole thing wasn't your idea."

"I know it was," Richard said. "But—"

"But nothing!" Arthur said. "I wasn't the one who decided we needed to traipse around the countryside, seeking heiresses. And I would have been happy to leave after that Mrs. Grubert incident. But no. You were the one who said we should stay."

"He's got a point," George said. "Richard, we've come too far now to give up."

Richard sighed. "Maybe I was wrong. Maybe this whole thing was a bad idea."

"Come on, man!" Arthur said, slamming his fist on the dining room table. "Where's your perseverance? Your sense of urgency? We need that money. We can't have those two frittering it away on guilty feelings!"

"What do you expect me to do?" Richard said. "It's not my money. It's Marianne's. She can do with it as she likes."

"Not if you persuade her to marry you," Arthur said. "I didn't see any charm happening. Where's your seductive prowess you brag about for no reason?"

"It died," Richard said.

Arthur sighed. "Richard, now is not the time to be a defeatist. George, tell him."

"Richard, what happened last night?" George said. "Did you manage anything?" This was his very sexist and clumsy way of referencing sex.

"No," Richard said, which wasn't entirely true. "I was a little distracted running for my life."

"That's no excuse," Arthur said. "You need to talk to her."

"Yes!" George said. "Make her see sense!"

"Maybe she already is seeing sense," Richard said. "Maybe this really is the best thing. The house is clearly off in some way. I'm not saying I fully believe in the ghosts and all that, but I'm not sure I want to set up camp here permanently, either."

"We need the money," George said. "Or have you forgotten? Has having a roof over your head the past few days made you soft?"

"Yes, all the relaxation and ease has rendered me an amnesiac," Richard said.

"Richard," George said, "you yourself said this was our last hope. Did you mean that or didn't you?"

Richard considered. "I meant it at the time," he said.

"Wonderful," Arthur said. "George and I will go occupy Madelyn, and you, Richard, will take Marianne out back, make wild love to her, and get her to forgo this insane scheme of giving away all her money!"

Arthur dragged George to his feet and they stood, waiting, until Richard reluctantly stood and began following them.

"This is futile," Richard said.

"Optimism, Richard, was never your forte," Arthur said. "But I have enough for both of us, and I know you can do this."

"Come on, Richard," George said. "If this doesn't work…we'll have to resort to drastic measures."

Richard sighed and followed them into the hall, which provided a clear view into Marianne's room, where Madelyn was busy explaining how best to situate a trunk. Marianne and Madelyn were currently talking over a pot of tea.

George and Arthur settled beside Madelyn. "So, Madelyn," Arthur said, interrupting casually and without remorse, "tell me about this new packing method."

Madelyn seized upon the conversation with enthusiasm. "Where do I start?"

"At the beginning, please," George said.

This left Marianne momentarily without a conversation partner, which enabled Richard to say, "Hamish wanted to show us something out back."

"Show us what?" Marianne said.

"Just something," Richard said.

"You'll forgive me if I'm rather untrusting given the last few days," Marianne said.

"I understand, but I think you'll like this," Richard said.

Marianne rose and followed Richard outside, where they wandered aimlessly around the overgrown topiary. "So what is it that Hamish wants to show us?" Marianne asked.

"Nothing. That was a lie to get you out here," Richard said.

"What for?" Marianne said.

"Nothing like a dead deer's head, if that's what you're wondering," Richard said. "I just wanted to talk to you. You know, normally. Without all the ghost and curse business. Just like two ordinary people."

"Like friends?" Marianne said. "Is that what we are?"

"I suppose not," Richard said. "But I do kind of like it out here." But he wasn't smiling.

"Is there something wrong?" Marianne asked. "I mean, aside from everything."

Richard hadn't planned to say what he was going to say next. He hadn't planned on saying anything in particular. Instead, it just kind of happened, that he said something true. "Last night… I'm sorry for last night, for how I acted. I suppose you felt I was endangering you by my actions." Then, he corrected himself. "I was endangering you by my actions."

"It's all right," Marianne said, but her voice sounded strained.

"I didn't mean—" he began, but Marianne shook her head.

"Let's not talk any more about that," she said. "Please."

They wandered aimlessly, in silence, for a minute. Then—

"You were right about my father," Richard said. "I do resent him, and my mother."

"What for?" Marianne asked. Richard sounded different than he had at first; he sounded sincere, and it intrigued her.

"For cutting me off without a penny," Richard said.

"Have you considered reconciliation?" Marianne asked.

"I've tried," Richard said. "But now I feel guilty that I tried."

Marianne was puzzled by this. "You feel guilty you tried to do the right thing?"

"But it might not have been the right thing," Richard said. "You see, my father isn't…he's not…" He sighed. "My father owns a plantation. Several, in fact."

"Oh," Marianne said. "I'm sorry."

"Yes, which is why all of this talk about…properties and rights and such has made me rather tense," Richard said. He seized a stick from the garden path and used it to mercilessly strike an errant stone into a scummy pond. "My father's cut me off. I pretend to be a gentleman, but I'm not really. Not anymore."

"He cut you off because you disagreed with him about the plantations?" Marianne asked.

Richard again, inexplicably, told the truth. "No," he said. "I wish that were the case, but it isn't. I mean, I wish I had quarreled with him over a matter of great moral importance, but instead I quarreled with him initially over a tract that I published in college. A tract on atheism, in fact."

"Oh," Marianne said, then she felt stupid. She felt all this merited a better response than "Oh."

"My mother," Richard said, "is very religious. Very Catholic, in fact." Marianne nodded.

"I knew she'd be upset," Richard said, "and she was. But she begged my father to forgive me, but he wouldn't. And I was young, and I said some things to both of them that were harsh, and I parted from them."

Marianne nodded.

Richard continued, and for some reason, felt as if his heart were pounding very fast and hard, even though he was only talking. "It wasn't until later that I learned that my father owned…owns several plantations. When I was a boy, he always told me that he meant for me to take over the family estates. But I never thought to ask what that entailed."

"How did you learn of it?" Marianne asked.

"I was in Paris, presenting on my theological ideas, when some good Samaritan"—here Richard snorted, in derision and irony—"brought up my father's business, I think to embarrass me. I pretended to have known, pretended that his indecency in that area had precipitated our rift. But it didn't. And when I confronted my father about it, he didn't deny anything.

He said that I was a fool, for never questioning how my schooling was paid for, or my carriages, or my clothes."

"When was this?" Marianne asked.

"Six, seven years ago," Richard said.

"Did your mother know?" Marianne said. "About the plantations?"

Richard snorted again. "Not only did she know, she approved. I thought I was enlightening her, when I wrote to her, telling her about my father's businesses. But she knew. Such a pious woman… And she knew that her donations to the church were coming straight from the fields of Antigua."

Marianne said, "Maybe she doesn't understand the implications of his business."

"She understands perfectly," Richard said. "And so do I. And yet, I wrote only a few weeks ago, to ask for more money, though I know exactly where it's from. They denied me, which I suppose, though painful at the time, is a relief now. It doesn't add to the burden of my guilt, at least."

Marianne was pensive. Richard appeared far away from himself, his hands occupied unconsciously with tearing leaves from shrubs and scattering them like papers. "Religious hypocrisy," she said finally, "is the one argument against religion I've never been able to counter effectively. The sins of religious people do more to harm the kingdom of heaven than all the devils in hell."

"Is that something your father says?" Richard asked.

"It's something I say," Marianne said. "Although I think he'd agree with me. He usually does."

Richard smiled a little. "Of course."

"Then you must understand," Marianne said, "why I need to give this inheritance up. Tainted money isn't much of an inheritance at all."

Richard nodded slowly. "But you're not to blame for what your ancestors did," he said. "For however they got this place."

"No," Marianne conceded. "And maybe, if not for nearly dying several times in the past two days, I would have kept the money or tried to give only part of it away. But waking up surrounded by fire felt a little too hellish for me. I have no desire to actually commit serious sins, and if I keep Rothmore and the money…well, maybe I'm complicit. Although," Marianne admitted, "I don't think giving away the money will keep me from having nightmares about this place. For such a beautiful old home, it's given me enough terrors for a lifetime." She shuddered, and Richard was overcome with a strong urge to—to do something. He didn't know what.

Richard had never laid out his parents' position, and thus his position, to anyone quite like that before. George and Arthur knew the gist of what he'd said to Marianne, but that knowledge had been acquired over years of surmising and living in close proximity, which made secrets hard to keep. Richard would have said he confided in George and Arthur. But he didn't usually confide in women. Not like that.

"It's easy talking to you," he said to Marianne. "It's like talking to a man."

"Is that a compliment?" Marianne asked. "Or an insult to other women?"

"Yes," Richard said. "Both."

"You know, most women are pretty sensible creatures once you're honest with them," Marianne said. "It's lying that tends to be so…offensive."

Richard considered. Was he lying? Had he been lying last night?

They had stopped walking and were now beside the pond. Though noon, the clouds had obscured most sunshine, and a light mist was falling. Richard could see drops forming on Marianne's lashes, trailing down her face in gleams. He remembered the attic and Marianne on the stool. And last night and her neck.

"I wish there were a stool out here," he said. "I would put you on it and take you off it again, and put you on it and—" He paused, feeling lost and awkward, but mostly very warm. Marianne was very warm, even though he wasn't touching her.

"Whatever for?" Marianne asked, looking at him with those lashes.

"Has anyone ever told you your eyes are luminous?" Richard said.

"No," Marianne said. "What does that mean?" But she knew what it meant.

"It means," Richard said, "that I want to kiss you."

Marianne blanched and, before Richard could say anything else, had blurted: "I know it was you at the opera!"

Richard paused in reaching for her. "What?"

"I know," Marianne said. "I know that at the opera, in London, you called me a hideous creature in a blue dress."

Richard was baffled. "When was this?"

"Last week," Marianne said. "I was at the opera, but we hadn't met yet, and you said I looked like a hideous creature, and that George was lucky to be half-blind, because then he wouldn't have to look at me."

"I'm sure I didn't say that," Richard said. "I didn't even know you a week ago."

"I know it was you," Marianne said. Were those raindrops on her face or tears? Richard couldn't discern between them. "I was wearing a blue dress, and sitting by my father, and you were leaving the opera with Arthur and George, and you said I was a hideous creature."

Richard's memory returned faintly. "I was at the opera in London, and I might have said not every girl there was pretty," he said, "but I'm sure I didn't use the word hideous."

"But that's what you meant," Marianne said.

"Marianne, I was leaving the opera because I couldn't stand all the strange looks we were getting," Richard said. "Looks from father's friends. And I may have made a crack about a clergyman, but that's just because I haven't always had good experiences with the church. If I said something about you, it was because I didn't know you. I was just…saying something stupid. And how do you know I was talking about you?"

"I know," Marianne said. "And I wouldn't say you were being stupid. Cruel, but not stupid. In fact, I would say you were being honest," she said. "For once."

"No, no I wasn't," Richard said. "I mean, maybe at the time I thought I was telling the truth, but that's not how I feel now. Not about you."

"Richard," Marianne said, touching his arm softly, "you don't have to lie to me. I understand. You don't find me handsome, and that's all right. It hurt my feelings at the time, in the opera, but I've forgiven you. You've saved my life twice. I can never repay you for that. I just, I know that you don't like me, in that way, and I want you to know that you don't have to lie."

"But I am not lying," Richard said, growing frustrated. "I was just being stupid when I said that, if I did say it. I meant nothing by it."

"You mean, you didn't intend for me to hear it," Marianne said, and there was no mistaking it now: those were tears on her face.

Richard could think of no reply—no adequate reply.

After taking a deep breath, Marianne smiled, but it was a watery smile. "I'm glad you were led to my door. I feel grateful to have learned that you're so much more than I initially thought you were. I am grateful we have come to understand each other. But please know that I don't mistake that mutual understanding for anything more. I expect nothing…"

"But do you want nothing more?" Richard asked, finally.

"I want honesty," Marianne said.

"And you think I'm lying," Richard said. "Or you think I'm incapable of honesty?"

Marianne wasn't sure what to respond. "I suppose," she said, "I think maybe you are lying to yourself, perhaps imagining attraction because it's convenient. But when all this is past, and I'm back in Dair, and you're back in London, you'll be glad you didn't act on this fleeting madness."

"So you think you're being noble?" Richard said.

"I think I'm being honest," Marianne said.

"Kiss me," Richard said, "and tell me I don't love you."

"Love?" Marianne said, shrinking away. "You don't love me."

"Prove that I don't," Richard said.

"I don't…how am I…" Marianne struggled within herself.

"Kiss me and prove that I am as indifferent to you as you say," Richard demanded.

"All right," she said, shrinking from refusal.

Richard took her head in his hands and kissed her. Marianne had never kissed anyone like this and found the experience startling. Afterward, she realized she was crying.

"Why are you crying?" Richard said, frustrated beyond words.

"Because I think you are a good man," Marianne said, "but I don't think your attraction to me, if it is real, is lasting. I think it's a result of a heated moment, a series of strange days. I can't demand anything of you based on that."

No one had ever called Richard a good man. Hearing her say that about him and mean it—it made him feel very warm, alarmingly warm. "You like me," Richard said, holding her very tight, "and you know you like me, and you're crying because you think you can't have me, but you do have me, you do, but you won't accept me. Why won't you accept me?" He wanted to shake her.

"Because," Marianne said, crying in earnest now, "we're not compatible in that way. You'll go back to London, and I'll go back to Dair. And I'll be a happy spinster, and you'll marry a nice, pretty heiress, and years later, we'll cross paths in the street, maybe in Bath, and smile a little, and think, 'What a strange time that was, at Rothmore,' and that will be it. People like us," she said, "they don't get married to each other."

"Why not?" Richard said, and he kissed her neck, and Marianne had a strong urge to slap him. How dare he touch her like that? Didn't he know she had to go back to living a normal life? Didn't he know she would always think of this moment? Didn't he know he was giving her strained and dangerous memories, which would complicate an otherwise seamless life of spinsterhood? How dare he complicate her with desire.

"I don't want that," Marianne said, pushing him away. "I don't want this."

Richard looked at her. "You don't want this because you think I'm lying to you? Or you don't want this because you can't stand a man looking at you in a way you can't predict and control?"

Marianne covered her eyes. "I don't know, I don't know."

Richard released Marianne and stood, briefly, staring at her with anger and frustration. Marianne had covered her face with her hands and could not see him looking at her. But she heard him leave, treading harshly on the grass.

Marianne sank onto the ground and cried for a long while. When she was done, she went inside, past the parlor where Madelyn and Arthur and George had moved, and where they were still debating the merits of various packing methods. Arthur and George, who had made almost as many hasty departures as Madelyn, had their own methods for swift exits, and the debate had become sincerely heated. Marianne ignored all this and went up to her room, where she collapsed on the stripped and sheetless bed and fell into a restless sleep.

"Marianne," Madelyn whispered.

Madelyn woke to find herself in the spare room, with Madelyn offering her a glass of water.

"You don't look so good," Madelyn said. "Did something happen?"

Marianne sniffled and then began to cry. "What's wrong?" Madelyn asked, now truly alarmed.

Marianne told her friend all that had transpired in the garden with Richard Lowell.

Madelyn was silent for a long while. "Marianne," she said at last, "does it ever occur to you that your pride will be the death of you?"

"My pride?" Marianne said. "I don't understand."

"You always think you've got things right," Madelyn said. "Even if you don't. And I don't blame you. After all, you are usually right. But not all the time."

"What's this got to do with Richard?" Marianne asked.

"You're so convinced he doesn't love you," Madelyn said. "But I've seen how he looks at you. I think he does care for you."

"No," Marianne said. "I don't...men don't see me like that."

"Like how?" Madelyn said.

"Romantically," Marianne said.

"This is what I mean," Madelyn said. "You get an idea in your head, and you won't change your mind for anything. I tell you, that man likes you."

"What do you know!" Marianne snapped. "You haven't seen me in years! And yet you tell me how to think about everything?" Then she felt ashamed for yelling at her friend. "I'm sorry," she said and began to cry again.

"Oh, Marianne," Madelyn said with a sigh. "What is it about you that you think men don't like?"

"Everything," Marianne said. "Everyone in Dair always said I was the plainest of my sisters."

"And you think those hicks are authorities on everything?" Madelyn said.

"They're not hicks," Marianne said.

Madelyn shook her head. "Marianne, I have been all around the world. I have seen all sorts of women. And you would be surprised at how many women, of all different shapes and sizes and appearances, manage to make men fall in love with them. People are funny like that. They all like different things."

Marianne sat on the bed, unsure what to think or say.

"Come on, come eat something," Madelyn said. "It's not as good as what your mother could make, but I think I've done all right."

Marianne nodded, collected herself, and followed Madelyn down the stairs. A small thought began to grow at the corner of her mind: What if Madelyn were right? What if Richard really did like her? In the terror of the previous night, the Midnight Mass gone awry, he had followed her. He could have run out of the house. He could have fled. But he hadn't. He had sought her out.

No, she thought quickly, shoving the thought into a corner. It was no use thinking like that. It was better not to be disappointed. It was better not to expect anything, then she would never be hurt.

Never mind that she was hurting right now.

Chapter Fourteen: Don't Eat the Stew

Richard could hear George and Arthur muttering. He turned over on the divan, on which he had fallen asleep. "You can stop conspiring," Richard said. "I'm awake now."

"You're not normally one to take afternoon naps," George said. "Did something particularly strenuous occur?"

"No, it didn't," Richard said. "Nothing happened."

"Then why did you come in the front door past noon, soaking wet and with a face like wrath?" Arthur said. "I take it that love making didn't go according to plan?"

"No, it didn't," Richard said.

"Could it be that you're actually having pangs of conscience about deceiving dear Miss Marianne?" Arthur said.

"Something like that," Richard said.

"Well, Madelyn says she and Marianne are leaving tomorrow morning for London to arrange things with the solicitor," George said. "So you have exactly one night to turn things around."

"No," Richard said. "I'm done with all that."

"Come on, Richard," Arthur said. "What was it you said about perseverance and charm winning the day?"

"I was a fool," Richard said.

"Don't worry about all that," George said, and his voice was strained in a way Richard couldn't identify. "Come eat some dinner. You'll feel differently once you have some stew in you."

"Stew?" Richard said, the promise of food shaking him momentarily from his black mood. "Where did you get stew?"

"Try some and guess," Arthur said. "Madelyn made it. Apparently being a missionary's daughter is the equivalent of learning to cook, clean, preach, read, exhort, and play the harpsichord."

"Quite a woman," George said.

"She is indeed," Arthur said. "Now, come on, what do you say to some stew?"

Richard nodded.

"Good boy," Arthur said, slapping his shoulders. "Come on, George. Let's not let our dinner get cold."

Richard followed them morosely, and his black mood was compounded, or rather reflected, by the weather. It had been only misting earlier, but now it was storming in earnest. Thick sheets of rain pounded the pavement, clearly visible through the windows. The sounds of thunder were constant, one crash barely resounding before the next.

Richard had a plan. He would studiously ignore Marianne, and she would ignore him, and they would enjoy their stew in silence. There was no need to examine his feelings, to wonder if what he'd said outside was a lie or the truth, to ask himself why he was so fixated on such a plain woman, even when the promise of money had been removed. There was no need to recall that moment, when he had wanted so badly to force her to love him, but for a reason he couldn't articulate. There was no reason to think about any of this.

When he arrived in the great hall, Richard was relieved to see that Marianne was absent. Madelyn was pouring stew into tureens. "It's not great," she said, "but it's food."

"Sounds great to me," Arthur said, clutching his silverware eagerly.

George appeared more skeptical. He unfolded his napkin slowly and sniffed and stirred the stew. "It needs a bit more salt, I think," he said.

"You're welcome to it," Madelyn said. "Add whatever you'd like."

George made a show of gathering the stew and taking it into the kitchen.

"He thinks living in poverty has given him experience cooking," Arthur said.

"Has it?" Madelyn said.

"No," Arthur said. "George is like a bear. He forages for his food."

"Are you like a bear?" Madelyn asked.

"No, Richard and I are more like magpies," Arthur said. "We love collecting shiny things. Shiny people, shiny places."

Richard nodded, although he had no idea what Arthur was saying. He was distracted by Marianne's entrance. Her face was blotchy and terrible. Perhaps she had been crying.

Richard decided not to think about that.

George reappeared, looking triumphant. "I think that gave it a nice flavor."

"Excellent," Madelyn said, spreading her napkin across her lap.

Richard couldn't help but notice Marianne fiddling with her spoon. Was she nervous?

Not that it mattered to him.

"Marianne and I will be leaving tomorrow," Madelyn said. "I went to the village and arranged the whole thing. It turns out, money is very useful for arranging things."

Marianne nodded. "We'll be leaving at daybreak," she said. "For London. I need to fix things with Mr. Poole about the distribution of the inheritance. Of course, he may not let me have any say in where the money goes, if I forfeit my hold on Rothmore, but I want to discuss it with him." Then she realized people were more intent on eating than listening, and she quieted.

Richard heard her voice as sort of distorted. Maybe it was residual tiredness that made the tablecloth seem redder than usual, the curtains a more striking shade of deep green. Was the stag on the wall staring at him?

Richard found he couldn't focus—his eyes were trying to convey to him what the plate in front of him looked like, but he couldn't see it. His head was pounding, and he—no, his head wasn't pounding. He only thought it was because he felt so short of breath. Why couldn't he breathe?

He looked over at Marianne, and her face swam into focus. She was so pretty. Why had he called her ugly? He couldn't recall. He had been upset about something having to do with her, but now he couldn't recall what it was. It didn't matter. He felt so happy about something, and he wanted to tell her. But when he opened his mouth, nothing came out. He tried to reach for the table, to take hold of something, because the world was becoming slippery, but he couldn't feel his arm or fingers. He saw them, sort of, but—

"What's happening to me?" he said.

"I don't feel right," Madelyn said.

"I think I'm gonna piss," Arthur said.

But all of this, Richard heard as if underwater. He felt himself falling, but didn't feel the impact, only knew that he was now looking at the ceiling. It was a very pretty ceiling, with a leafy motif that some monk must have labored to carve.

Marianne? he thought. Had she fallen also?

And then, over him, he saw a face that was familiar. But who was it? Richard squinted, really trying to focus, but it was hard, so hard. There was light on the other person's glasses, and the candles kept reflecting off it darkly.

"All right, old friend," George said. "Time to pick up where you failed."

Richard knew something was wrong, but he couldn't bring himself to feel any sense of urgency. "What's happened?" he said. But the speech was a bit garbled.

"I didn't understand that," George said, "but rest assured, you'll all recover." He held up a vial. "Tincture of opiate," George said, "can have desultory effects, particularly on the uninitiated."

Richard tried to ask a question, but it evaded him.

"You're probably wondering why I'm doing this," George said. "But all that will be made clear."

George stepped over Richard and took a woman, a woman who looked familiar, by the arm, and began tugging her into another room. Richard knew he knew her. Perhaps it was her blue dress. There was something important about her. But he couldn't muster the strength or will to move, and besides, the ceiling was swooping toward him so quickly, and he felt—

He felt better than he ever had before, so happy.

So why did he know he was in more trouble than he'd ever been in before?

Marianne was being guided by a man whose glasses fascinated her. The pretty reflections on them were very nice, and she tried to grasp them, but couldn't. Holding a candle aloft in one hand, and with her in another, George made his way up the stairs and into the library. Progress was slow, because Marianne wasn't steady on her feet, but they arrived eventually.

"Ms. Keyes," George said, setting her down on a divan. "I need your keys."

Marianne laughed. "Keyes giving you keys! Funny!" Everything was funny.

"Yes, yes," George said, but he didn't seem as amused as Marianne felt. No, not amused—deeply, deeply elated. "You were given a key to your great-uncle's collection. Now where is it?"

"I don't remember," Marianne said, staring at a lock of her hair in between her fingers. She had a split end. So sad. But she didn't feel sad. She felt happy.

George grabbed her shoulders and shook Marianne. "Think! Where is it?" He sighed. "I knew I shouldn't have given you any laudanum."

Marianne struggled to remember. Someone had said something to her about keys.

"I think—" she said. "In my pocket."

George shoved his hand into her skirt and extracted a large pocket, untying it from her waist expertly. Marianne watched as he poured out its contents on the ground, seizing a key.

"Now, where is it?" he asked.

"Where's what?" Marianne asked. She was still holding a lock of her hair.

"The collection," George said. "Your great-uncle's secret collection."

Marianne thought a while, but it was too hard. Why was George being so loud? Why wasn't he as content as she was?

"I don't know," she said.

George stared at her. "You have to know."

"I can't think right now," Marianne said.

George sighed, stepped back, and then swung very hard, slapping Marianne across the face.

He was a large man and swung hard, and Marianne knew her face hurt very much, but it didn't upset her. She only felt the site of the blow with a hand and asked, without concern, "What was that for?"

"Because I need you to remember," George said. "Where is your great-uncle's collection?"

Wait—hadn't Mrs. Grubert once said something about that? "In there," Marianne said, pointing vaguely at a bust on a shelf.

George turned instantly, chucked away the bust—"So long, Cato," he said—and inserted the key in a small compartment underneath. It clicked open, revealing some coins.

"Shiny," Marianne said.

George had begun to sweat, but now he was sweating and smiling. Very strange, Marianne thought. But it didn't bother her. Nothing did.

"So these are the famed Cuban coins," George breathed.

"Just old coins," Marianne said.

"Not just old coins," George said, facing her. He couldn't seem to resist talking at her about his victory. "These are pure silver, the last remnants of the Spanish conquistadores. Worth a fortune, if you know the right buyer." He carefully placed them in his handkerchief and tucked them inside his coat pocket.

"So now you're happy?" Marianne asked.

"Happiness has passed me by. But am I satisfied? Yes," George said.

"That's good," Marianne said. "But it'd be better if you were happy." She was.

"Tell me how easy it is to be happy when your only friend ostracizes you from your family and acquaintances," George said, "drags you around the world, rewards you with nothing, and refuses even to commit to his plans of seducing an heiress and stealing her inheritance."

"I'm an heiress," Marianne said.

"That's the point," George said.

"Is it?" Marianne said. She thought back to the strange incidents of the past days, but without feeling any of the dread or fear she had experienced at the time. "Were you all going to steal my money?"

"Yes, but through legal methods. Marriage, in fact."

"I'm not getting married," Marianne said.

"Yes, I know," George said. "Richard failed me, again. But for the last time. I have learned, at last," he said, "that the only person a man can trust is himself. When my family cut me off, I should have learned it. When my fiancée rejected me for losing my money, I should have learned it. But it's only been lately that I have truly learned my lesson… If you want something in this world, you have to seize it with both hands. If not through legal means, then illegal. Everyone has a right to provide for himself."

"But why do you want coins?" Marianne asked.

George sighed, and began looking around the room. At last he grabbed the bust of Cato. "Because," he said, setting the candle down and holding the bust with both of his rather large hands. "Because the cost of reentry to society is gold, or, in my case, silver, and the older the silver, and the more blood on it, the more it's worth. If I can prove they're as old as I think they are—" He grinned in self-satisfaction. The light reflected from his glasses in the otherwise dark room, and Marianne thought of old depictions of hell she had seen. The thought was funny to her.

"The beauty of it is," George said, "with all the strange goings-on here, and with no witnesses left, no one will know I was ever at Rothmore. They'll chalk up your disappearance to yet another mystery of the estate."

"Those coins could be cursed," Marianne said, but the thought didn't bother her. She thought only "curse" was such a funny word to pronounce. So strange and funny. But wasn't everything?

"What's cursed is poverty," George said. "And I don't intend to have that curse anymore."

He raised the bust of Cato, and Marianne thought, "he's going to bash my head in," but the thought didn't bother her. Nothing bothered her anymore.

Chapter Fifteen: Benefits of Too Much Time in Vienna

Richard became aware that he was on the floor and that this was not comfortable. He sat up, feeling strange but oddly happy.

Arthur was beside him, though slumped over his stew, not on the floor. That woman—Madelyn—was looking around, pupils constricted and eyes rather unfocused.

Someone was missing.

"Where's Marianne?" Richard asked.

"Upstairs," Madelyn said.

"Where's George?" Richard asked, and a cold feeling began to settle around his sternum.

"I think he went with her," Madelyn said. Then she slumped forward, landing heavily on the table.

Richard sighed and shifted Arthur's head off of the plate, so he didn't accidentally drown in soup, then went out of the room in search of Marianne.

His limbs still felt strange, but Richard made it up the stairs without making much noise. Then he crept along the dark hall, feeling for the walls with outstretched hands. Then he saw, along the floor, a glimmer of light in the gap between floor and door: someone was in the library. Richard got down on his hands and knees and looked in the gap and saw familiar feet: George's shoes, which had been abroad and back, barely held together with mud and string; Marianne's, much neater and smaller.

Richard entered the library to see George, holding aloft a bust of—was that Cato?

"Put Cato down, George," Richard said, his heart sinking.

"Hi, Richard," Marianne said brightly.

"You?" George said, blinking at Richard. "I gave you enough opium to knock out an elephant. How are you functioning?"

"George, you forget that I spent a summer in Vienna having entirely too much fun," Richard said. "I built up quite a tolerance to the opiate family."

Richard realized the trajectory of George's arm; it was almost as if he'd intended to hit Marianne Keyes in the head with a heavy bust.

George sighed. "That is one of the numerous disadvantages of being your friend, Richard. You're so full of surprises."

"Why are you standing like that?" Richard asked. "What are you doing alone with Marianne?"

"He was getting Great Uncle's silver," Marianne said, sounding very cheerful, albeit somewhat garbled.

"She's right," George said. "I'm stealing the old man's silver and leaving this wretched place."

"Without me?" Richard said. "And what about Arthur?"

"I'm tired of traipsing along behind you two," George said. "It's exhausting being friends with intellectuals. They have so many ideas, but so little funds."

"George, we're friends, aren't we?" Richard said. "We've been through so much together."

"I think our friendship is at an end," George said.

"Then just take the silver," Richard said. "Why are you…what does Marianne have to do with this?"

"I can't have her telling tales about me, can I?" said George.

"So you're going to, what? Kill her?" Richard said. His mouth felt very dry, even saying the words.

"You make it sound so much worse than what you were planning to do," George said. "Marry her, steal her money, break her heart—all of that is acceptable, gentlemanly behavior. But to kill her? Now that's too much. According to Richard Lowell, at least."

Marianne looked between the two men, obviously struggling to comprehend through the stupor of opium what was being said. "You were going to break my heart?" she asked Richard, still smiling.

"No," Richard said. "Not anymore. I decided that that wouldn't be a very nice thing to do."

George sighed. "So you had some pangs of conscience. How inconvenient for you."

"I'll get over it," Richard said.

"You might," George said. "Or you could come with me. We could split the silver, split the money, get back on our feet. Wouldn't it be nice to spit in our families' faces?"

"What about Marianne?" Richard asked.

"What do you care what happens to her?" George said.

"I just don't believe in murdering young women," Richard said. "Until recently, I would have thought we were in agreement about that."

"All of this talk about belief with you," George said. "All those speeches and tracts handed out at salons and universities about what's right and wrong, and what God is or isn't. But don't you get it? No one cares what you believe or don't believe, Richard. They only care if you have money or not. And now you don't, and I do." George reached into his pants and extracted a large pistol. Richard's heart sank.

"I care," Marianne said.

"What?" George said.

"I care what Richard believes," Marianne said, still smiling absently.

"Shut up," George said. "Come on, Richard, think about it: you and me, with money in our pockets, taking Europe by storm. Doesn't that sound nice?"

"Somehow, I believe her more than I believe you," Richard said. "I don't think you would share the money and even if you did, I wouldn't take it. I've had enough of blood money."

"Your loss, then," George said, raising the pistol to point at Marianne. "I wanted to do this differently. A gunshot doesn't make a murder scene feel very sublime, does it? But needs must."

Richard didn't really think about what happened next. He didn't have time to. Instead, he leapt in front of Marianne as if his life, rather than hers, depended on it, thinking nothing, and registering only a very sharp, nigh on excruciating, pain in his collarbone, before falling to the ground in a very unheroic heap.

George let out a cry of frustration. "Damn you, Richard!"

And then, behind George came the sound of shattering glass. Richard saw the window exploding inward, and a bearded man step through, mallet in hand. With one swift blow, the groundskeeper had dispatched George, who fell to the carpet, groaning, his head no doubt aching.

"I saw the light," Hamish said as calmly as if he were introducing himself at afternoon tea. "I feared another fire, so I got my ladder and climbed up."

"I'm glad you did," Richard said, then began to cough violently.

"Aye, you look in need of a doctor," Hamish said.

"You're right again," Richard said when he could breathe.

"Richard, you don't look well," Marianne said.

"Remember me better than I deserve," Richard said. Was he dying? Probably. "I did love you, in my way."

And Richard fainted from loss of blood.

Richard awoke twice in the carriage ride to the village, but quickly faded again into unconsciousness.

Then he arrived at an inn, where he was deposited on a strange bed, and a series of strangers came in and out of the room. Then there was another strange man looming over him, looking disappointed. Was it God?

No. God wouldn't have shoved his finger inside Richard's collarbone.

"I can't get it," the stranger said, his sweat landing on Richard's face. "The skin's swollen shut."

Then, Richard was aware of cursing very loudly as the equivalent of a silver stick was rammed repeatedly into his body.

"Got it!" the doctor said, extracting first a bloody strip of linen and then, with another silver instrument, what may once have been a bullet, but which was now so covered in blood, it was not recognizable. "He's lucky. The bullet didn't go too deep. The pistol may have malfunctioned."

Richard must have been screaming. He only knew that, however, when someone put the mouth of a bottle in between his teeth, and the sound stopped.

Someone tipped Richard's head back, poured brandy down his throat, and Richard managed to swallow before fading yet again.

Richard woke gradually.

"Try not to move," a female voice said.

Richard blinked. Gradually, a face came into focus.

"Marianne," he said. His voice was groggy. "What day is it?"

"Two days since your surgery," Marianne said. "And you're at the village inn. I've paid for the room for the week. I have enough money left for that."

Richard realized that his arm was trussed up, held in place by a series of knots. "What's all this?" he said.

"The doctor said you can't move your arm until it heals," Marianne said.

"How long will that take?" Richard asked.

"Didn't say," Marianne said.

"What if I have to pee?" Richard said.

"You already have," Marianne said. "I changed the sheets. I had to change your clothes, too. Sorry about that."

Richard sighed. "Hopefully, it wasn't too much of an education for you."

"I'm a clergyman's daughter, not a nun," Marianne said. "I've done my fair share of nursing before."

"Right," Richard said. "I'm always underestimating you."

Marianne shrugged. "It's understandable, I suppose."

"Marianne, there's something I have to tell you," Richard said.

Marianne looked at him expectantly.

Before his courage evaporated, Richard had to tell her: "I didn't come to Rothmore because I was assaulted by highwaymen."

"I know that," Marianne said.

Richard sighed. "When I read in the paper about your inheritance, I determined to try to worm my way into your life, to deceive you, to marry you, and to get you to sign over your inheritance to me." It didn't sound any better out loud than it had in his head. "I didn't mean for it to go as badly as it went. What George did is…unforgivable. And what I did was awful."

"Your plan didn't work," Marianne said.

"No," Richard said. "It turns out, I'm much less charming than I thought, and not as good at stealing from people."

"Maybe that's a good thing," Marianne said.

Richard looked at the ceiling. "I understand if you never want to see or speak to me again."

Marianne nodded slowly. "Maybe I should, but you did save my life three times. Hamish told me about what you did in the library. My memories from that night are…blurry."

"I saved your life only two times," Richard said. "The fire and the gunshot, I'll accept. But you weren't technically in mortal danger from the severed deer head. That was just unsettling."

"Very unsettling," Marianne said. "I can still smell that animal on me."

"Are you going back to your home?" Richard asked.

"Yes," Marianne said. "When I wrote and told my father and mother everything that had happened, they demanded I come home. Apparently, Rothmore is too dangerous. Even for ten thousand pounds."

"You were going to give it up anyway," Richard said.

"Yes," Marianne said. "I don't want blood money. And besides, my parents can take care of me. I'll be a burden, but better a living burden than independent and dead."

"What about Rothmore?" Richard said.

"I haven't spoken in person to Mr. Poole yet," Marianne said, "but I don't think the estate is mine, not if I forfeit the inheritance. It may just remain empty for the present."

"That doesn't seem fair," Richard said.

Marianne shrugged.

Richard sighed. "You seem very calm about all this."

"I've had time to think about everything," Marianne said. "And I think everything's worked out for the best. I'll go back to Dair. You'll go back to your life. George will, well, George will be in Newgate. It seems that stealing silver and trying to shoot someone are punishable offenses."

"Have you seen him?" Richard asked.

"No," Marianne said. "Do you want to see him? They haven't transported him yet."

Richard thought about it. "No," he decided. "I don't."

Marianne nodded.

"What about Arthur? And your friend?" Richard asked.

"Arthur woke up from a very good nap two days ago," Marianne said, "and had to be apprised of the whole situation. He was very shocked, needless to say, but has chosen to remain with you at the inn for the length of your convalescence. He's asleep now in the next room. Madelyn has gone ahead of me to my parents' house. She was very excited that she now has a good story to add to her missionary adventures. She says she's already started writing the novel."

Richard looked at the ceiling. His skin itched. He wished for more brandy, but he had a sense that Marianne wouldn't approve.

"Marianne," Richard said at last. "I'm so sorry. I'm so sorry about all this."

Marianne's matter-of-fact tone had faded, a little, when she said, "It's all right."

"It is not," Richard said.

"I admit," Marianne said, and Richard knew that she was speaking differently now—more softly, from vulnerability. "I admit that I, briefly, felt angry about what happened outside"—Richard knew she meant what had happened in the garden—"when I learned your real intention had been to trick me into marriage. But I can't be too angry with the man who saved my life, twice. No one who jumps in front of a bullet meant for someone else can be all bad."

Richard stared at the ceiling. "Marianne," he said, "I'm so sorry for what I said at the opera. If it's any consolation, I'm kind of an idiot."

Marianne smiled faintly. "You did get yourself shot." Then, her smile faded. "You're not an idiot, Richard. Just cruel, sometimes. I think you could be a very good man, if you let yourself."

Richard laughed, and it hurt. So that was why they had told him not to move. When the pain stopped pulsing behind his eyelids, he managed: "It requires money to be a good man. Poor men have to scheme and lie."

"Not always," Marianne said. "I think you could find a way. You could do anything you want."

"You will make someone a very good wife," Richard said.

"No," Marianne said. "I suspect I'm not the marrying type. You're the only one who has even thought about offering, and that was when I had money. Besides," she said, probably to distract from any self-pity in the sentiment, and smiling a little again, "it would be very hard for someone to impress me. I would expect him to save my life at least three or four times. He'd have to outdo your record."

"Are you staying at the inn?" Richard asked.

"Not anymore," Marianne said. "My mother and father have demanded my immediate return home. In fact, the coach was supposed to leave a few minutes ago."

"You should go make sure it's still there," Richard said.

Marianne nodded and stood, but still she hesitated.

"I wish I could have tricked you into marrying me," Richard said. "Who knows, maybe we would have actually been happy."

"I don't think relationships built on lies work that way," Marianne said. Then she softened. "But yes, maybe that would have been nice, for a while."

Marianne went to the door. "Goodbye, Richard."

It wasn't until after the door had shut behind her, that Richard had mustered the courage to say: "Wait."

But it was too late.

Chapter Sixteen: Return

Everyone was very nice to Marianne when she returned to Dair. Her parents hadn't yet rearranged the rooms, so Marianne went right back to sleeping in her childhood bedroom as she had before. Her parents didn't ask her about what had happened at Rothmore. Apparently, her letter had been detailed enough to satisfy their curiosity.

Only Mr. Keyes brought it up, at breakfast. Marianne was eating, and her sisters were making their usual amount of noise. Amid the din, Mr. Keyes looked at Marianne and said, "I'm so sorry for letting you go there alone."

"It's all right, Dad," Marianne said. She was startled to see her father blinking away tears. "Dad?" she said.

Mr. Keyes blinked rapidly and went back to eating his eggs.

And the breakfast resumed as usual. And that was all that was said. Mrs. Keyes was relieved to have another pair of hands to help with the never ending chores around the parsonage, and Marianne happily disappeared into the work, although sometimes, she could be caught not at her work, staring into space, and sighing. When Mrs. Keyes would ask whatever was the matter, Marianne couldn't bring herself to say the truth, that she was remembering what it had felt like to kiss Richard Lowell, and instead made up lies about being tired.

Madelyn stayed with the Keyes family for three weeks and during that time received regular correspondence from Arthur, who reported that Richard's wound was healing, against all odds. Sometimes, Marianne wanted to ask Madelyn if Arthur ever mentioned something about Richard's plans. She wondered if Richard ever thought of her, if there was any truth to what he had said in the garden at Rothmore. But she decided that was too ridiculous a thing to ask.

She had thought, for a moment, about insisting on staying with him. He had needed someone to take care of him while he healed. But she had decided that would imply some expectation on her part, perhaps a romantic expectation. Which she didn't have, had never had.

Soph had asked, once, when Marianne was climbing into bed: "Did you like him?"

"Like who?" Marianne asked. She blew out the candle, and the room descended into dark.

"The young gentleman who was with you at Rothmore."

"No, he tried to shoot me," Marianne said.

"Not that one," Soph said, and Marianne could feel her rolling her eyes. "The other one. That Richard one Madelyn was talking about."

Marianne considered. "Yes," she said. "I liked him a lot. But the feeling wasn't mutual."

"Oh," Soph said. "I didn't know that could happen."

"Sometimes, it happens," Marianne said. "But it all worked out for the best. Aren't you glad I'm back?"

"A little," Soph said, exhibiting the younger sister's reluctance to admit any fondness for her siblings.

Marianne kissed the top of her head, then rolled over quickly. She didn't want Soph to notice that her eyes weren't dry.

When Marianne had been back at the parsonage for six months, she was surprised when her mother called to her from inside the house: "Marianne," Mrs. Keyes said. "You have a visitor."

"Is it Mr. Poole?" Marianne said. She had been working in the garden and was smeared in dirt. She rose, brushing off her hands. She had been expecting the solicitor, with whom she had some residual business. Her great-uncle's inheritance had been put in a trust, a sort of financial limbo, given her refusal of it, which apparently required a great deal of paperwork. Because of her refusal to travel to London again, Mr. Poole had to come to her.

"No, not this time," Mrs. Keyes said.

"Hello, Marianne," a familiar voice said.

Marianne turned, a sensation like dread and excitement overwhelming her. She managed to keep her face without expression only through a lifetime of feigning passivity. "Richard!" she managed.

"Hi, Marianne," Richard said. He had improved his mustache since she'd last seen him. She was startled to see he was not wearing a sling.

Mrs. Keyes lingered, watching as Richard strode across the lawn to where Marianne was standing. Marianne saw her mother's eyes on them. "Would you like to go for a walk?" Marianne asked.

"A walk would be good," Richard said.

They went through the garden fence and passed into the lane. "Your shoulder looks better," Marianne said.

"Yes," Richard said. "The doctor said the nerves will never fully heal, but I still have a good range of motion, which is nothing short of miraculous."

"Thank God," Marianne said. She wasn't sure what to do with her hands and folded them across her chest. "How's Arthur?"

"In London," Richard said. "Didn't Madelyn tell you?"

Marianne shook her head. "Tell me what?"

"Apparently he and Madelyn are preparing to go on some missionary voyage to Africa," Richard said.

"I thought Arthur was an atheist," Marianne said.

"He is," Richard said. "He's spreading the gospel of atheism. He'll probably have more luck than I ever did. Madelyn says this is a perfect chance for an experiment. Apparently they have a competition over how many people they can each convert."

"Oh," Marianne said. "That sounds like Madelyn. She likes a challenge."

"Do you?" Richard said.

"No," Marianne said. "My life here is very tranquil." There was no need to tell him of all the nights she had tossed and turned, thinking of him. Then, "Aren't you going with him? Arthur? I would think that sort of adventure would appeal to you."

"The thing is," Richard said, after a pause, "I'm not sure my convictions are as fixed as they once were. Getting shot tends to have that effect, I suppose."

"What convictions?" Marianne asked.

"My religious convictions," Richard said. "When I was in that inn, I kept thinking, again and again, how unlikely it was that I would survive. How unlikely it was that the bullet didn't do more damage. And then I survived. What do I know, maybe there is a God."

"I could have told you that," Marianne said. "Without getting shot."

"Yes," Richard said. "I guess so."

They were silent for a while. Marianne felt nervous, but she didn't know why. They were just old acquaintances, talking about mutual friends. Then Richard cleared his throat.

"It's really very lovely country around here," Richard said. "Very green."

"Yes," Marianne said. "Though there are no grand estates around here. Nothing like Rothmore."

"Maybe that's a good thing," Richard said.

Marianne nodded. "Less hauntings, certainly."

"Marianne," Richard said. "I wanted to talk about, that is, I wanted to ask you—"

Marianne had continued walking, but Richard had stopped, and he grabbed her arm. "Marianne," he said. "Could we forget Rothmore for a moment? If I were just a man, meeting you for the first time, and you had never met me, knew nothing of me, of my faults and failings and mess of a past, would you even consider me?"

"Consider you as what?" Marianne asked.

"Consider marrying me," Richard said.

"But I do know you," Marianne said, trying to sound light yet unaffected. "And I know you don't love me. Not in that way."

"But you can't know that," Richard said, "because it's not true. I do love you."

"Richard—" Marianne began.

"Marianne," he said. "Please, I will let you talk, but please, please listen to me. I have had three months in an inn, most of which was spent in very uncomfortable reflection on my life. And I have had another three months of frantic activity, trying to get some sort of a place for myself in London—some kind of honest work, if you can believe it. And in all that time, I never got you out of my mind."

"You just need to meet another woman," Marianne said, and she was embarrassed by how fragile her voice sounded.

"I have met other women," Richard said. "London is full of them. And they're lovely. Wonderful. And I've been across Europe. The women there are also lovely. Good times were had by all. But I have never wanted to be anyone's husband but yours."

Marianne struggled to keep herself steady, to moderate her feelings, which were becoming unruly. "Richard," she said, "we had some very shocking experiences together at Rothmore, but I beg you not to mistake excitement for affection—"

"Damn it, Marianne!" Richard said. "Why is it so hard for you to believe I love you?"

"Because I have nothing to offer you," Marianne said. "I have no inheritance. It's gone. I forfeited it."

"I don't care," Richard said. "I don't care about that. I want…you. I want to know…do you…could you…is there any situation or world in which you could love me?"

Marianne tore away from Richard's grip and began walking very quickly to the end of the lane. Richard swore, then hurried after her.

"Marianne! Marianne!" he said.

Marianne had sat down, heavily, behind a tree.

"Marianne!" Richard said, spotting her dirt-streaked dress. He knelt in front of her. "If you don't want me, just tell me. I'll leave you alone. I'll never bother you again."

Marianne stared at him. "I do want you," she said, at last, "but I'm just… I'm just a clergyman's daughter. I'm not exciting. I'm not beautiful. I'm scared that I'll love you, and you'll grow bored of me, and then—"

"You want me?" Richard said. He had stopped listening after hearing that.

Marianne nodded.

"Really?" Richard said.

Marianne nodded again. "But what if—"

"Then there is a God!" Richard said, and he kissed Marianne so thoroughly and for so long, Mrs. Keyes began to miss Marianne and sent Soph, Anne, and Evie in search of their older sister.

Richard was interrupted in his love making (which was, finally, going well) by a chorus of giggling. He looked around to see three young girls, bearing a resemblance to Marianne, cackling at the sight of him and their sister together.

Richard peeled himself off Marianne. "Your family's found us," he said, brushing his hair back into place.

"Oh," Marianne said, and she couldn't keep her face from flushing crimson.

"Gross," Soph said, wrinkling her nose.

"Marianne," Evie said, giggling wildly, "you were kissing that strange man! You have to get married now." (Evie was, as always, a clergyman's daughter and had a very strict sense of how these things worked.)

"All right," Marianne said.

"Really?" Richard said.

Marianne nodded.

And the couple fell to kissing again, until the three younger sisters were thoroughly disgusted, as all younger sisters are by their older siblings' love lives, and begged Richard and Marianne to keep their affections to themselves.

When the three sisters had chaperoned Marianne and Richard back to the parsonage, and told everyone in their family and the village that Marianne was marrying a man who had come to call, it was the second strangest piece of news regarding Marianne Keyes that the village had heard that year.

"We wish her well," the neighbors said. "After that inheritance business went nowhere, the girl deserves some happiness."

And Marianne quite agreed.

Chapter Seventeen: Epilogue

Marianne Keyes and Richard Lowell were married shortly. After attempting a reconciliation with his parents that immediately turned sour when it became clear Marianne had no money, and Richard had no intention of involving himself in the family business, Richard decided to go into business for himself and became a well-respected publisher. He found it as ironic as anyone that his best-selling publication was a translation of the bible. Marianne, for her part, became a writer of ghost stories, which brought her some degree of fame. They enjoyed frequent visits from Marianne's sisters, and their friends: Arthur and Madelyn, who had many more adventures. Marianne Keyes gave Richard nine children, all of whom learned, from an early age, never to insult someone at the opera; they might just end up marrying that person later on.

Mr. Keyes did not at first approve of Richard Lowell, thinking his daughter much too good for the washed-up son of a slave owner. (Which she probably was.) But Richard, through his diligent efforts and evident respect for Marianne, and his virtues as a husband and father, proved himself worthy of Mrs. Keyes' and Mr. Keyes' deep love and regard.

Marianne, for her part, did not become boring to Richard, and her beauty, which had at first been well hidden, grew as she aged, rather than faded. By the time they married, Marianne and Richard could both confidently say that they each thought the other the most beautiful and interesting person in the world.

Rothmore was never sold and eventually fell into ruin after several tenants reported strange goings-on and hauntings. Sometimes, stories of those occurrences reached Marianne and Richard. "Rothmore may still be haunted," Marianne was wont to say, at which Richard would kiss her and say:

"Thank God. Maybe it will bring some other couple together yet."

About the Author

Micah Cozzens is primarily a poet, a graduate of Ohio University's Creative Writing PhD program. Her poetic work has appeared in *LIT magazine*, *Segullah*, and *Fugue*. Her first full length poetry collection will be released in 2026 from By Common Consent Press. *The Heiress of Rothmore Hall* is her first published novel. She is currently working on a second poetry collection about Karens, Princesses cleaning bathrooms, and the Kardashians. Follow her at over-poetry.com or via Instagram @micahcozzens. She would love to talk to you about her nephews, nieces, religion, chocolate, teaching writing, yoga, and/or your writing. She is always on the hunt for fantastic new books to enjoy and praise—including yours.

www.ingramcontent.com/pod-product-compliance
Lightning Source LLC
Chambersburg PA
CBHW071533100726
47908CB00004B/1376